CEMETERIES
ARE FOR DYING

By William L. Story

CEMETERIES ARE FOR DYING
DOMINO SPILL

CEMETERIES
ARE FOR DYING

WILLIAM L. STORY

PUBLISHED FOR THE CRIME CLUB BY
DOUBLEDAY & COMPANY, INC.
GARDEN CITY, NEW YORK
1982

All of the characters in this book
are fictitious, and any resemblance
to actual persons, living or dead,
is purely coincidental.

Library of Congress Cataloging in Publication Data

Story, William L.
    Cemeteries are for dying.

    I. Title.
    PS3569.T6554C4   813'.54
    ISBN 0-385-18190-6   AACR2
Library of Congress Catalog Card Number 82-45078

This book is dedicated to my wife, Marie,
and to my children, Suzanne and David.

I would like to acknowledge the following people whose information was helpful in the writing of *Cemeteries Are for Dying:*

        Sgt. Jerry Bellew, PPD
        Sgt. John Tivey, PPD
        George Michaud
        Dave Sinclair

I would like to make special acknowledgment to my agent, Chuck Taylor, whose advice and criticism were invaluable.

CEMETERIES
ARE FOR DYING

CHAPTER 1

Well into her third and final lap, Alison Bradley was finally over her fear of running in the cemetery at night. The place had proven innocent, just as she had known it would before she had actually started her run. When she had left her Datsun on the street, however, and was actually in the cemetery, her pulse fluttered and she found herself swallowing rapidly several times.

She would have turned around but recollection of Doug's taunts made her hold her ground and begin the series of stretching exercises that preceded a run. She had forced herself to do them slowly, deliberately, and methodically.

Through the skeletal tree branches, the early November moon, a stingy slice, gave little light, mostly a faint glow off the patches of white frost.

As she got into the process of running, of feeling legs, lungs, and heart functioning smoothly, her fear faded to caution and, now, as she was nearly through, became exhilaration.

She laughed at her fears. At thirty-two, she should be above them. Ghosts, goblins, vampires, et al. existed only in Stephen King novels and overwrought imaginations—certainly not in the real world. Not even in a cemetery at night. Alison did acknowledge the possibility of danger from boozed-up kids or winos but she would be watchful: She was confident she could outrun them.

Oh, that Doug had been something. She had never seen the chauvinistic side of him—which, she thought, just proves that you never really know someone fully, not even someone you've been living with for so long. What a stupid thing it had been. The two of them acted like little kids.

"You wouldn't dare run in the cemetery at night," he had said, referring to the cemetery that the two of them ran in together during the day.

She remembered she had laughed at the ludicrousness of the taunt but also at something else. At fright. An image of the cemetery at night, jutting tombstones and menacing shadows conjured a deep fear that had raised the short hairs on her neck.

But, too quickly, she had said, "I would too. I would too dare."

And so it had gone. The dare, the double dare, prompted by a stupid argument. Well, here she was, doing what Doug had said she would never dare do. And it was easy, so easy. Wait till she told him.

She was on the incline past the pond that marked the last part of the mile-and-a-half loop when she saw the flickering light in a dip toward the center of the cemetery. She hadn't noticed it on the first two laps.

Curious, she marked its approximate location. Was it an eternal flame? That would be a discovery that would impress Doug. She could hear herself telling him as a casual afterthought, "Oh, guess what I saw while I was running at the cemetery? An eternal flame. I never knew there was one there, did you? Of course, you wouldn't notice it during the day."

She finished her lap and, for her cool-off walk, headed toward the center of the cemetery, to where she had seen the light.

Alex Harris was coming back from the small, any-denomination chapel where he had been making sure that everything was going all right with Harold when he saw Alison peering from behind a bush at the men refilling the grave they had dug up, emptied, and refilled. They were working by lantern and its flickering flames made their shadows large and vague. He snuck up behind her and smashed his fist into the side of her head, just in front of her right ear. Without a sound, she collapsed at his feet to the semi-frozen, lumpy turf.

He looked at her a moment. She was certainly old enough to know better than to be skulking around like this. She was quite pretty. Her eyes were half shut and unseeing, her lips slightly parted. Despite the cold, a thin sheen of perspiration glistened on her forehead. He noticed her running shoes and sweat suit. What kind of fool would run here at night?

He bent down and picked her up, cradling her almost tenderly. Her breathing was shallow and raspy. He had hit her hard. He wished he had hit her harder but he couldn't bring himself to hit her again. No matter. She was out, probably seriously hurt. Harold would finish things up.

He carried her back into the old castle-like chapel, Gothic-looking and gargoyled, down the stairs, and set her on the stainless-steel rolling table in front of the crematory ovens. He checked her again. If anything, her breathing was shallower and more spasmodic. She wouldn't wake. This was a damn shame but it had to be done.

He went around the corner to get Harold, who had just emptied one of the ovens.

Harold Parkins held up two stained, stubby fingers and Eddie the barkeep poured him a double shooter of cheap rye. Harold usually had just one after working late, and usually he managed to nurse it for fifteen minutes, long enough to sustain an exchange of monosyllabically grunted opinions with Eddie on the enduring topics of sports and weather.

Tonight, though, with an unsteady hand, he downed the double in under ten seconds and signaled for another. Eddie, if surprised at this departure from habit, did not show it except, after pouring, to position himself in a friendly, receptive way near Harold in case he wanted to talk.

Eddie believed in fulfilling the bartender's classic role of being a sympathetic listener. A man could iron out a lot of problems by just talking about them with the help of a little amber and it sure as hell was a lot cheaper than a trip to the shrink. Those bastards would just keep you coming, sitting there sucking a pipe, legs crossed like a fairy, squinting and nodding like they were in pain or had to fart. Eddie knew. He'd gone to one for a while after coming home from Korea but it did no good. He'd straightened himself out in the end. But he could recognize when a man was bothered by something and old Harold without a doubt was flapping around inside.

Harold worked on his second double a little more cautiously. Already, the warmth of the first had spread commendably from his gullet to his torso. He tried to concentrate on the flickering TV screen over Eddie's shoulder. One of the UHF channels was showing an old Steve McQueen movie. The color was too intense and Steve glowed a rich pink.

It had been a real pisser tonight, not at all the kind of situation that Harold had ever anticipated having to handle. Ordinarily, he and the other guys did nothing more than some digging and hiding stuff and kept their mouths shut because they were very well paid and it was all under the table. Uncle Sugar never got his mitts on it.

Oh, sure, maybe half a dozen, eight times over the past five years or so, since they started this new deal, he had had to work the ovens for the guys who paid them. But they were already dead, the ones who had been brought in. And they were scum anyway. You could tell. To get involved with the boys who did the dropping off, they had to be scum. Involved in a different way from how he himself was. He just rendered a service, mopped up after the fact.

But tonight had been really different, unique in three ways.

Number one, it had been a woman. A very pretty young woman that they brought down to him.

Number two, it was the first time Alex had brought someone to the cellar. Alex said that she had been nosing around and had seen too much. They couldn't take a chance. Alex made the decision on his own. Said that *they* would order the same thing. They had no choice.

"Do your thing, Harold," Alex had said, just as if he was telling him to take out the trash.

Harold gulped the rest of his second shooter. He tried to focus on Steve McQueen but could make no sense out of what was happening on the screen. He knew he wasn't going to get any sleep this night.

Eddie was saying something. Harold had a hard time differentiating between Eddie, who was looking at him strangely, and Steve McQueen, tight-lipped, who was driving like a maniac.

Harold knew he had to get out of there, had to get home, had to *walk* home to clear his head, had to drive the pretty young woman away, the woman whose face was getting in the way of Eddie and Steve McQueen, and the whiskey wasn't working, wasn't living up to the promise of its early glow.

He swore to himself that he hadn't known at first, because, if he had, he could never have done it. He punched the side of his face to drive her from his mind and, zombie-like, got off the stool, nearly falling. He had to get out of here before he screamed.

Because number three, and worst of all, she had woken up and reached out and touched his hand just before he had put her in the oven.

CHAPTER 2

Peter Swann held his ground between two swooping taxis. He downshifted to second, tromped hard on the accelerator, and the almost fifteen-year-old 420 Jaguar sedan easily beat out the cabs, crossed Beacon Street, and was back on Charles.

He tried to suppress a little-boy grin of exhilaration and then gave in to it. The car could hop and he loved it. Loved it despite its frailties: the heater was a cold draft, a noisy one at that; the Lucas gauges had the consistency of cobwebs—speedometer and odometer had retired at 36,000 miles, oil pressure, coolant temp, and battery wavered and flickered beyond anything comprehensible. The tachometer alone remained loyal.

But the car was sexual. The Jaguar body divine. The faithless gauges were a beautiful white-on-black set in a dashboard of real walnut spangled with a row of toggle switches. The looks, feel, and smell of red leather seats intoxicated Peter.

He checked over his shoulder, pulled into the right lane, and turned up Mount Vernon. He knew he was a cliché: crew-neck sweater almost hiding button-down collar, driving a Jag sedan to his apartment on Beacon Hill. But no matter, contentment doesn't spring exclusively from originality.

He parked in the semicircle of driveway, its two entrances punctuated with a wrought-iron fence whose elegance was a bit diminished by some broken peaks. It had taken a real effort to break those peaks and Peter often marveled at the indefatigable lengths that petty vandalism could go to. His apartment—old, brick, a nice blend of respectability and bohemian avant-garde—was typical of the charm of Beacon Hill, a charm that endured years of transient student populations and, more recently, both minor and serious crime.

Inside, the apartment was cold. Its energy efficiency was no better than the Jaguar's, a price apparently that went with this type of chic.

Peter's cat, Clark, a black-and-white fluff, tilted against Peter's legs, tail high, rubbing and turning his body, insistent that he be Peter's first priority. From the cabinet over the kitchen sink, Peter took a small green can with a fancy name and fed the cat. Clark had developed rather connoisseur tastes for one not too long removed from the alley.

He toyed with the idea of starting the fire in the fireplace but settled for the quartz heater. Tonight during dinner here with Nancy he'd throw the thermostat up to seventy to offset the heat loss of the fireplace. Romance at well over a buck a gallon.

Placing the heater in the doorway of the small kitchen, he got a bottle of Labatt's from the refrigerator and set it on the counter by the window. It was almost dark out, the clear November sky spattered with masses of low clouds. The scene suited Peter. He liked the seasons, the changes. And he liked them to be as they should be. November should be dark and chill, tinged with melancholy. It should give meaning to staying inside and finding light and warmth from fireside and friends.

He took a box of Ritz crackers from the bag of groceries he had brought in. Crushed, mixed with butter and herbs, they would be the stuffing for the shrimp. Baked stuffed shrimp and sirloins broiled over the gas grill, baked potato, a salad, wine, crème de menthe parfaits. Unimaginative, Peter conceded, but satisfactory.

Peter was content. He anticipated the evening. He would enjoy preparing the meal. Even more, he would enjoy sharing it and the evening with Nancy. Things were going well of late and this evening was to be savored.

The phone rang. He answered. It was Doug Symonds.

"Pete, you busy?"

"No, not really. Just fixing up some chow for tonight. I've always got time for you. You know that, Dougie."

The peculiar lump that Peter felt in his throat whenever he talked with Doug Symonds felt bigger than usual, for Peter knew what the call was about and felt depressed. He could tell from Doug's tone that it was about Alison Bradley, Doug's girl, and that it wasn't good news.

"Still no word on Alison?"

"Nothing." There was a pause. "That's the thing. Not knowing. The police still think she just took off."

There was another pause. "That doesn't make any sense to me, Peter. Does it to you?"

That was a tough one. A specific yes or no didn't leave much room for hope.

"Look, Dougie, what's it been, just over a week?" Verbalizing it was bad, and even though Peter kept his tone light, the words spoke for themselves.

"You sound like the cops. Nothing's the matter. Happens all the time, they say."

"I—"

"But they forget one thing, Peter."

"What's that?"

"We weren't married."

"I don't—"

"It's when you're married that the old lady or the guy goes out for the proverbial loaf of bread and never comes back. There was none of that with Alison and me. We had it together, you know that, Pete."

"Yeah."

"Pete?"

"Doug, I want you to come over here tonight. I'm going to cook up some steak and shrimp for Nance and me and there's plenty." There was still time to go out for more.

Doug started to protest.

"I won't take no for an answer," Peter said. "You need to talk with someone. I need to talk with you."

"Pete, I didn't call for that. I just wanted to talk for a minute with someone on the phone."

"I know you didn't, but I insist you come. Alison means a lot to me too. You know that."

After he hung up, Peter sat in the kitchen for a while. He was deeply troubled by the phone call. Alison had not been seen for over a week and he felt in his heart that something was horribly wrong. For both Doug and Alison, he had a very special feeling, a feeling even stronger than for family. He wished he could do something to help.

He owed them his life.

The bullet had caught Peter in front of the left shoulder below the collarbone. It was no mere flesh wound. The spreading warmth soon became a deep cold and he felt himself giving in to the blackness that was starting to enshroud him. Vaguely, he knew that Doug was kneeling beside him, pressing into his shoulder, trying to stop the gush of blood.

"Hang on, Pete. Hang on. Don't quit on me."

All that he remembered before blacking out was Doug throwing him over his shoulders and somehow carrying him away from the North Vietnamese regulars who had scattered the rest of their squad in a savage fire fight.

Doug Symonds was the last person he remembered when he fell unconscious. He was in shock by the time a copter got him to the field hospital and it was a near thing for a while.

He awoke three days later in a hospital in Saigon to the classic disorientation of not remembering what had happened or knowing where he was. Alison Bradley was the first person he saw. He had never seen her before, but she became a security against his confusion.

"How are you doing?" she said, smiling, bending over him. Her prettiness to him was beauty, her gentle manner, strength. She held his hand for a while and washed his face with a cool cloth.

Through his recovery, Alison was there until he rejoined his company in less than a month.

He knew that Doug had saved him in the field, and it was from Doug that he learned much later that Alison had at one point saved him in the hospital when he almost slipped away while still unconscious.

They met, Doug and Alison, when Doug got permission to visit his wounded friend at the hospital.

The three of them finished their tours in Nam and returned home to Boston. Doug and Peter got teaching jobs at the same suburban high school. Alison continued her nursing at a Boston hospital.

The bonds that held them in Vietnam grew even stronger back home.

The gloom of November would not be staved off by the burning logs or flickering candles. The dinner had been excellent, but Doug Symonds' despair and Peter's empathy were too deep. Faltering attempts at small talk failed to elevate the mood and now they sat, Peter, Doug, and Nancy Brewer, fiddling with the crème de menthe parfaits.

"You know, it was so stupid. I feel like a fool," Doug said, staring into his parfait.

Peter swallowed a spoonful of ice cream. "What do you mean?"

"Well, the night Alison disappeared. We had a . . . not exactly an argument. I mean, it was really stupid."

This was what Peter was waiting to hear. He didn't know any of the specifics of Alison Bradley's disappearance nine days ago, and close as he was to them, hadn't wanted to intrude. He had assumed that the matter was personal. But Doug's phone call had implied otherwise.

"You know how Alison is about being independent. A real feminist." Doug toyed with his spoon, then drained his glass of wine.

Peter refilled it.

"Well, anyway, we got into this discussion of bravery—this

sounds so juvenile—bravery and strength. It all started because Alison is bent out of shape about something at the hospital. One of the male nurses gave her a hard time about nurses unionizing. Said female nurses didn't have enough guts to stand up for their rights, or something like that. Don't ask me how, but the conversation turned into a discussion of male-female bravery and from there into running at . . . this is so damn adolescent-sounding. We got into an 'I dare you' routine."

"About what?" Peter said. "You said something about running."

"Yeah. I told her that she wouldn't dare run in the cemetery at night." Doug's face reddened. "It was kind of a thing with us. When we'd run it together during the day, we'd often kid about running it at night."

"Which cemetery? Oak Way?" Peter asked.

Doug nodded. "I didn't think she would. I just said that she wouldn't dare to. I don't even know if she did. I had a Parents' Night meeting, remember those, Peter?" Doug said, gamely trying a little humor. Peter didn't teach anymore, not since he had won the state lottery. "I was at school and was going to meet Alison at nine-thirty at the Magic Pan. She never showed.

"To make a long story short, her car and her running stuff are the only things missing. Besides her, of course." He made a small gesture with his hand. "It seems obvious to me that she went to the cemetery or intended to go. That's something she'd do just to prove a point." Doug looked from Peter to Nancy. He was their age, early thirties, athletic, trim, but now obviously shaken.

"What do the police say?" Nancy asked.

"Naturally, they checked out the cemetery, but, like I told Pete on the phone, they think there's a good chance she just took off." He swirled the wine in his glass a moment, then drained it all. "No body. No sign of foul play. But I don't buy that she just took off. I mean, number one, I *know* Alison and I know she wouldn't up and take off. Jesus, you live with a person and you just *know* certain things. Number two, who the hell would pull a fade in running shoes and sweat suit?"

Peter and Nancy studied the remnants of their parfaits. Finally Peter said, "Doug, you don't seem to be leaving many options."

"Just two. Either she did take off, which means I never knew her, or . . ." He grimaced. "Or something happened to her at that cemetery."

The wind whistled in the fireplace and the flames spangled a bright orange.

"I can't help blaming myself. At night, there's no telling who the hell's in that cemetery. Winos, weirdos, kids on drugs." Doug poured himself more wine. "I'm sorry. I'm not good company tonight. I probably ruined your dinner."

Peter sat, pensive, brooding, rejecting the notion of something sinister happening to Alison, the angel in the hospital.

Doug finished his wine and stood up. "I appreciate the dinner and the sympathetic ears. They really helped."

Nancy reached out and touched his arm.

Slowly, Peter looked up. "Doug, you stay here tonight. I've got a sleeper sofa. I want you to stay."

Doug came around the table and clapped Peter's shoulder. "Thanks, buddy." He shook his head. "But no. I want to go someplace and think."

Peter saw him to the door. When he came back to the table, the dark of November didn't seem just a romantic backdrop to Nancy and the fire.

CHAPTER 3

Americo Scalise was nervous, a nervousness composed of very contradictory feelings: elation and fear. Elation for the promise of what his plan held and fear that if he failed it would be the ball game. These guys played hard ball, played tackle. But he wasn't going to blow it. He had planned too long and too carefully. He had covered himself every step of the way, had made all the necessary arrangements, and he'd be gone two days before he was due to turn in his receipts. He and Angie would be safe in a new place with new names and even, in a short time, new appearances. A little facial surgery (appointments all set up and no questions asked—that's what plenty of dough could do), change the hair a bit, a stache, maybe a beard for him, and they'd be new people. A warm climate, a lot of money, but best of all, no more being a gofer, because, despite the new job about a year ago, let's call a spade a spade, he thought, that's what I still am, a piddling gofer. Oh, sure, he'd been moved up, big deal. It was dead end. Peaked, at fifty-three. It was risky but worth it. Good things don't come cheap.

Risky? Oh, shit, risky was too, too tame a word. A screw-up and it would be permanent enshrinement as part of a lamp stanchion in some shopping center or in a bridge abutment to be dug out two or three thousand years down the road like some Egyptian mummy.

He knew he had to stop thinking like this. That's what makes you screw up. Be grateful for the new job which lets you hold receipts for two weeks before handing them in. Those two weeks' worth are going to make up for all those years of running around collecting and every day turning in what had been collected. Now I'm the guy, he thought, that those other schmucks hand over to every day and worry about pissing off or I'll have their ass. Be grateful for the changeover from turning in receipts every week to every two weeks as part of a streamlining process just like the big corporations get into.

It was that extra week's receipts which gave Americo the idea about six months ago. Two weeks' receipts was a tidy sum. A tidy sum indeed. And it showed real trust to let a guy hold it for two weeks. But he'd earned the trust. He'd been a true and loyal soldier for too many years, and even though there were no complaints about the living (it sure as hell beat being a working slob), he'd never get to where the real dough and fancy lifestyle was.

Unless he made the move himself. And he was going to. And for that he felt nothing but pure joy.

Americo paid his fifteen cents on the bottom span of the Tobin Bridge and tromped hard on the accelerator of the new Lincoln. Geez, the car had no pep. Goddam Ayrabs. Smaller cars, smaller engines, it was all their fault. Try to keep up, get a new car every year, and the thing had all the piss wrung out of it. No matter. Pretty soon he'd be parlaying a lot of dough into a lot more dough. Visions of a Mercedes-Benz, maybe even a Rolls.

He took the off ramp to Chelsea and headed for his produce store. It was almost dark and time to collect the day's receipts. He thought of the girl he'd just left. A bit younger than he usually got, probably not even twenty, but real good. He needed girls regularly. Especially lately to help kill the tension. That's all they were. Therapy. No attachments. They'd never take Angie's place as far as feelings went. That was the thing. With most guys who fooled around, there were no feelings left. But as far as he was concerned, there would never be anyone to take Angie's place. He was sure that Angie didn't know about the girls and he took great pains to make sure she never found out.

He nudged the heater up a notch. Climate control sucked. You could end up freezing your ass off while it regulated itself. One thing he wouldn't miss was the New England winter. Pretty soon it would be endless summer, year-round tan and frosty drinks. He smiled and settled back comfortably in the leather seat as he drove the narrow, winding streets. There was no way he hadn't made the right decision. Why stay around here like some kind of glorified collection boy making believe Revere Beach or Nahant in the summer was Miami and in the winter busting away for a couple of weeks to suck up the rays and making believe the rest of the winter you didn't care as long as the Celtics or Bruins were doing okay.

He was still smiling as he pulled up and parked in the loading zone in front of Ricky's Fresh Fruit and Vegetables. Inside, through the steamy windows, he could see the two kids who came there to work part-time after school. They couldn't steal much, he thought wryly. Probably stuff their faces with grapes or apples, but turnip and squash isn't too big with the teen set. He knew they took turns smoking their brains out in the storage room when he wasn't around and maybe dipped into the till a little even though he paid them well enough. But who gave a shit? This place was nickel and dime.

They'll jump when they spot me coming, he thought as he got out of the Lincoln.

"Hi, Mr. Scalise," they said, pretending to be busy with brooms and loading bins all of a sudden as he pushed past them and heads of lettuce and sacks of potatoes to the back room. There were no customers.

He turned on the same FM station he'd been listening to in the car. Dentist office Muzak. A touch of class.

Then he went to the safe. As he twirled the knob, he was struck, as always, by the irony of this action. Very few would dare think of even fooling around with the money in the safe. Even desperate, doped-up freaks. They knew whose money it was and how efficient were their methods of detection, interrogation, and punishment.

Americo shuddered a bit as the nervousness returned. But he was no doped-up crazy. He was part of that which others feared and he knew how it worked. He would strike from within and be long gone before they knew of the defection.

Tonight, he'd tell Angie. There'd be no problem there. She'd go wherever he went with no questions. Christ, she was good that way. None of that liberation crap. He hadn't told her yet because that was just one more potential leak. Not that she'd blab or consciously do anything to jeopardize things, but still she was a woman and all it might take was just a remark.

She'd miss her brother, might even feel guilty about him getting some heat from what he and Angie did. But no real problem there. He was a big shot, not far down the ladder from number one. As a matter of fact, he got Americo the job, but it took him long enough. But you couldn't throw your life away worrying about a brother-in-law's ass.

He took an empty money box from the safe. Twelve others, each containing . . . Oh, God, his heart jumped as he again counted and multiplied numbers he knew by heart.

A noise from the store startled him and he withdrew his hands from the box guiltily, then laughed at his own nervousness. What the hell, it was just the two kids working. Probably dropped the potatoes. Besides, at this point he wasn't doing anything he shouldn't.

He put the empty box on the table in front of him and calculated what today's receipts would bring the total to. He smiled. With money like that, only a fool could fail to secure a base of ease, independence, and, yes, power.

He marveled that they would allow one man to have so much of this money for so long before turning it in. But he knew the reason. Disbelief. Disbelief that an insider—family, actually—would violate the code. And fear. His. A fear that should be so strong that it would dispel any temptation, any toying with notions of transgression.

But he'd show them. He'd be his own man, unafraid. Because at fifty-three a man has to do certain things.

He unwrapped a Garcia y Vega and poured himself a glass of red wine. Then he took out his list to check off the names as they came in with their day's take. Drop-offs were two hours, between five and seven. When you remembered they were just about his total workday, where was the complaint? The complaint was, well—he'd been through that in his mind about ten million times.

Drop-offs in his area were of three types: gambling of various categories, drug sales, and sex, which included prostitution and porn. Each group got forty minutes and usually it went pretty smoothly, almost to the minute. Occasionally, he got involved as middleman on proceeds from B and E and auto theft, but not usually. That was another ball game, and returns, while big, could be sporadic.

He tilted his chair back, rocking slightly as he sucked on his cigar and absently hummed a background to the radio. John Denver. Nice. Fresh air and sunshine, which he'd be enjoying pretty soon.

It was a bit too early for returns, so when the door opened he was surprised. His heart skipped, then beat a tattoo when he saw Carmine Bubblegum and Louie Ciuccio. The room spun crazily, his chair nearly tipped, and John Denver went sour.

Where had he slipped up?

"Sorry, Ricky." Carmine's voice was gentle and apologetic, at variance with his huge body and swarthy pirate's face. The piece in his hand glinted coldly.

"Mike is gonna be collecting for you today. We're going for a little spin, but finish your wine first."

"What—?"

"You screwed up, Ricky. Geez, you had a nice setup and you got hungry. Dumb. You shoulda stayed away from the broads. Got your old lady nervous as a bastard. She was worried about you and talked to her brother. So we been watching you and it was easy to figure you was going to take us for a ride. We only look dumb, Ricky. You ought to know that."

Americo drained his glass of wine and fought a moment's battle with his fear, which threatened to go out of control. He must remain cool. It was demanded, part of the code. He'd be damned if he'd stain his pants.

"Look, you guys, there's more dough here than you'll ever earn being muscle. How about a three-way split?" As he spoke the words, he knew they were useless. But he kept his voice businesslike. He would not beg.

"Let's go, Ricky," Carmine said softly. "We'll go out the back door."

They rode in silence. Americo had lost his battle with fear and didn't trust his voice to speak. He knew the old policy of leaving bodies to be found as a warning had been changed. There would be no trace of him. He couldn't come to grips with the concept of his own oblivion and was still grappling with it when the car pulled past iron gates into a sepulchral darkness.

He had a minute to wonder where he was before Carmine helped him from the car. And his vague, fleeting impression of a castle was shattered by the .357 magnum slug that destroyed his brain.

Alex got the word about three o'clock in the afternoon. It came as a phone call while he was in his office, a small, vine-covered brick building, rather quaint, like something from a fairy tale. He went outside to his old, beat-up green Ford pickup and drove to Bridge Pond, where Harold was supposedly working. For a moment, he couldn't locate him but that was nothing unusual with any of these guys when they were doing their routine, legitimate stuff. What the hell could you expect from someone who got paid in shit? No wonder these guys often took a little nap in the bushes during the day. Nothing wrong with that but not in this weather. Too goddam cold.

But that's why this other deal was so nice. A real good supplement to the regular check. He laughed. Usually it beat their regular paycheck.

He thought, as he often did, back to that day five summers ago. It had been a big affair, over fifty cars easy. When the ceremony was over, he and the boys, who had been discreetly out of sight in the background, moved in. They hadn't been working more than ten minutes when a long black Caddy returned. Nothing unusual about a Caddy here, but this one, he could tell, was privately owned and he didn't recognize it.

Nor did he recognize the short man who got out of the back seat. Everything about him said money. Money and something else too. And it didn't take Alex long to define that something else. Power. From his clothes and manner to the driver of the Caddy, this short, sallow man in his fifties, maybe sixties, with the white hair that had obviously once been black, exuded authority.

He had come up to where they were working and asked who was in charge. He led Alex away from the others, away from the Caddy, out of earshot behind a beauty bush in the glory of its full bloom.

They had talked for a few moments. It had mainly been a feeling-out process, friendly and general, but the man arranged to talk to Alex later. He had said he'd get in touch. When he did—it wasn't more than a week later—he laid out just part of his offer. It was very simple, and Alex found it extremely attractive. But he admitted to himself that he had also been a little fearful to refuse.

Gradually, the deal took on new wrinkles but never anything they couldn't handle. And the dough was always there. Cash. Never had to quibble, never had to wait. Really, the only requirement was silence. They all got the message on that. At first, he thought there might be some difficulty there, but good money and a guess about who they were dealing with took care of that. The short man was very generous but also very persuasive about the need for absolute discretion.

That's why Alex was a little worried about Harold. Since that thing with the girl, he hadn't been right. Harold normally didn't have a hell of a lot to say and that bothered Alex. He had no escape valve.

Shit, he didn't feel good about the girl either but it wasn't the usual job—not by a long shot. He had done the hardest part. What the hell was Harold in an uproar about? All he had to do was work the ovens.

Well, this job tonight was more like the usual stuff. No doubt some wop who had been a bad boy. They'd bring him in dead and Harold would pop him in the oven so that there would never be a trace.

This return to normalcy might be good for Harold, might steady him. Kind of a reassurance that the business with the girl was freakish. One of those unfortunate things that happen and everybody regrets. Christ, what the hell did Harold think that he, Alex, was? Some kind of monster?

He found him under one of the huge European beech trees. *Fagus sylvatica*. Alex knew all the trees, all the shrubs, by their fancy, scientific names as well as by their regular names. Beeches were real beauties with their smooth-as-skin light gray bark that kids loved to initial.

Harold was just staring into the scummy water that had partially frozen around the edges. He had a small pile of leaves and twigs raked together. An afternoon's work.

"Jesus, Harold, slow down, huh," Alex said, looking at the small pile. He knew the poor joke was wasted as he said it. Harold had no sense of humor. He clapped him on the back to let him know the comment was light, not a criticism.

"How you doing, boy?" To Alex, Harold fell into that category of things that could be called boy. Kids, dogs, and dumb old geezers.

Harold shrugged and poked at the ground with his rake, making a few tentative scratches at some leaves stuck to the frozen ground. Despite the frost, decay and humus perfumed the air.

"You feeling okay?"

Harold scratched some more. "I feel okay."

"That's good. I worry about you, you know." Alex regarded him closely. The pouches under his eyes seemed more pronounced than usual. The stocky figure slouched. The stained chino work pants hung loosely, belted low, below the gut.

"Harold, how many years to retirement?"

Harold chewed on something, maybe his cheek. "Little over two."

"Hey, that's great." With his boot, Alex nudged a stick wedged into the ground. "You been saving up some of that extra dough? You know, to help out the old social security. Sweet deal, it'll really help."

"Yeah." The tone was unenthusiastic.

"Thatta boy. A guy needs all the help he can get today, huh?"

Harold shrugged again. "Yeah."

Alex began to feel exasperation. Harold was no conversationalist. If he couldn't tell when a guy was trying to be nice to him, well, frig him. If he wanted to stand around feeling sorry for himself, that was okay, but he'd better not screw up this deal for everyone else.

"Got another little job tonight."

Harold slowly turned and looked at Alex. "What kind, digging?"

"No. Your kind, you know. But not like with the girl. I mean, this one will already have been taken care of."

"Oh. Not just a swap?"

"No, but what's the problem? This has got nothing to do with us. I mean, it's not like we could do anything to stop it. And who gives a shit? You know the kind of scum they bring in."

"Yeah."

"It'll be just you and me. Sometime between five and five-thirty. I'll have the gates open. You have things ready downstairs."

Harold scratched at the ground but didn't answer. He was chewing at his cheek again.

"You got that?"

"Yeah."

Alex turned to go, but Harold put a big hand on his arm. "I don't want no more like that girl."

"None of us do, Harold."

CHAPTER 4

The morning was clear. Cars and pedestrians going to work plumed clouds of white moisture into the cold air as they attacked the day.

Peter Swann was in the midst of the traffic near Government Center and Quincy Market. The Jaguar's twin-overhead-cam six burbled pleasant, resonant sounds. It hadn't balked too badly this morning when he started it, but something would have to be done about that heater. Benumbed extremities were a high price for automotive sensuality.

The traffic didn't bother Peter; in fact, he enjoyed Boston's commuter Grand Prix with its deserved reputation as a test of nerve and skill. Not so long ago, such traffic would have turned his stomach to acid and knots if he was combating it to beat a time-clock deadline.

But since winning the lottery, he knew if he had the smarts not to overextend himself, he could live the good life without hassles and tribulations. A few indulgences like the Beacon Hill apartment, the Jaguar, premium beer and wine, he could now easily afford. And without work. At least not until or unless he felt like it. What that work might eventually be, he had not yet decided.

Traffic suddenly broke and Peter popped the clutch and stepped hard on the accelerator. The Jaguar shot a gap and Peter intimidated an oncoming car with Montana plates as he crossed traffic for a left turn. On impulse, he maneuvered a quick U-turn to pick up a vacant spot across from Faneuil Hall. He locked the Jaguar and leaned against it absorbing the incongruities of Quincy Market and Haymarket Square.

Across from him, in the plaza between Faneuil Hall and Quincy Market, two remnants from an era of almost twenty years ago were rendering their versions of Bob Dylan sounds. One slapped a tambourine and tried to sound nasal while the other slid a harmonica back and forth across his mouth like a shiny ear of corn. They were bundled in pea jackets. Long, straggly hair hung limply from wool stocking caps. Peter wondered about them for a moment. Diehards of a vanishing breed or precursors of the resurrection of an old order? He didn't know.

To his left and around the corner, vendors with their pushcarts of produce spilling onto the streets scratched the air as they hawked their wares, jumbling their sounds with those from the duet. It was a concert in stereo and strangely pleasant.

Peter strolled.

"Hey, fancy Macs, here. Whadda ya say, friend? Look at these apples. Nice. Real nice."

Peter nodded and smiled and slipped past the vying vendors to the pedestrian tunnel that would take him to the North End and his morning coffee at Sam's.

He scooted across traffic and headed down Hanover Street, congealed with knots of double-parked cars. The cluster in front of Sam's was particularly heavy and seemed vulnerable to the traffic it threatened to close except that an empty Boston police cruiser idling at the rear fringe acted like a protective shepherd.

Inside Sam's was the usual crowd that to Peter seemed right out of something by Damon Runyon or Jimmy Breslin. The place was thick with people, smoke, and noise and smelled of coffee and pastry.

Steaming Styrofoam cups of coffee with a generous shot from a V.O. bottle lined one end of the counter while a few cups of plain coffee dotted the other end.

Pete took one of the plain, left fifty cents on the counter, nodded to a busy Sam, and moved to one of the chrome-and-plastic tables that were once modern but now were tacky.

Peter couldn't put his finger on it, but it seemed there was a somber, restrained mood about the place this morning.

With his foot, Joey Angelli—Joey Blowtorch—pushed a chair out for Peter. "Pete, baby."

"Joey. Barbie." As usual, Barbie Melons was seated with Joey. Peter had never gotten her real last name. He sat with them and seasoned his coffee with milk and sugar.

"Gotta tell you a story, Peter." Peter knew Joey would have a story. He seldom wasted time with preliminaries and the stories were invariably colorful, the news of the street, but the distinction between truth and fantasy was often blurred.

Short, thin, rather hunched, in his fifties, Joey leaned across the table. He cradled his cup with strong, sensitive fingers. "Remember the trouble the neighborhood was having with them goddarn Dobermans?"

Peter nodded. He vaguely recalled that some of the young studs in their early twenties, guys with short-bed pickups with mag wheels and the inevitable skittering Dobermans, had been involved in neighborhood complaints of the dogs nipping at little kids or old grannies.

"We complained to those guys I don't know how many times. Real nice and polite. Like 'Hey, you guys, can you keep your dogs under control? Lots of little kids around and older people and the dogs nip and make everyone real nervous.' Especially by Paul Revere Park, the Prato. You try to sit on a bench and there's always these guys with their big Dobermans with the spiky collars and all. I mean, you can't relax, you're sitting on a bench and one of them things comes up and stares at you or sniffs your leg or something. One time, one of them damn near took a leak on me."

Joey sipped from his cup and squeegeed his lips together as if he found the liquid distasteful. "Like I say, a bunch of us, real polite, have asked them a thousand times to watch the dogs. So, Tuesday—Monday?—was it Monday, Barbie?"

"Monday," Barbie Melons said. Also somewhere in her fifties, Barbie Melons, once the possessor of a glorious body, had turned amorphous.

"So, Monday, one of the dogs takes a nip at Tony Jack-knife's kid, he's about eight or nine."

"Nine," said Barbie Melons, finishing her coffee. Peter could smell the cheap whiskey on her breath. Everyone knew that Sam bought cheap generic booze and put it in the fancy V.O. jug with the ribbon on it. At a buck a cup, he did all right on the coffee, especially never having to bother with a liquor license.

"You guys want more coffee?" Barbie Melons asked.

"Yeah, get me one, Barbie," Joey said. Peter shook his head no.

"Wait'll she comes back, I'll finish," Joey said. He nodded to the two cops who came out of a back room and grabbed a couple of coffees from the dollar side of the counter. One reached over the counter and clapped a friendly hand on Sam's shoulder and said something. The two cops and Sam laughed mirthlessly and the cops took their coffees outside to their cruiser.

Barbie Melons brought two coffees back, sat down, and adjusted the natural assets that had given her her nickname and now threatened her with curvature of the spine.

"Real cold out," she said. "Need a couple of cups today."

"Like I was saying," Joey continued, "Monday, one of them goddarn Dobermans takes a nip at Tony's little kid. Right on the leg. Not real bad but the kid has to go to the hospital for stitches and shots. What'd he get, Barbie, twelve, fifteen stitches?"

"Twelve. Got a couple of bad gashes, poor little kid. Actually, he's a pain in the ass," Barbie added, "but he don't deserve to get bit."

"So that does it. I mean, now everyone's really pissed off. We tried telling these kids nice but they don't listen. Not like the old days when the kids showed respect. These kids don't work regular, don't contribute. I mean, they could move into some nice deals but all they want are those trucks and good times. So, I think this is for the best because they got to be taught a lesson. They got to be shown what this neighborhood can do."

Peter sipped at his coffee and regarded Joey Blowtorch. The man was obviously building up to what he saw as an example of the kind of justice that the power structure of the neighborhood could mete out.

Joey leaned forward and lowered his voice. "This morning, what do you think were piled up under Paul Revere's statue near where Tony's kid got bit?"

Peter made an expression that said: I don't know.

"Now get this, there were fifteen—fifteen, that right, Barbie?"

"Fifteen."

"There was fifteen dead Dobermans all piled up. All stiff as a goddarn board."

Peter let his breath out through his teeth.

"I kid you not. Fifteen dead Doberman pinschers piled under Paul Revere."

Peter wondered about the logistics of the thing. Had a hit man lined the dogs up against a wall and mowed them down with a machine gun? Ground glass in hamburger? Were the dogs lured or just taken by force from their masters? It was quite a feat and disbelief must have shown on Peter's face.

"Don't ask me how," Joey said. "I didn't believe it when I heard it, so I tooled down to the park and saw the goddarn things with my own eyes. And I saw a couple of those wise guys loading them on a pickup truck. No complaints from them either. They got the point, no question."

Peter wondered whether he was being put on. Probably not. What would the point be? He pondered it a moment. He felt bad for the dogs but had to admire the accomplishment as a real touch. Carrying it out must have been difficult and only a dullard would fail to be impressed with the efficiency and organization of the thing.

"Yeah, it was a busy night, all right," Joey was saying. With his finger, he beckoned Peter to lean his head forward. His tone became quiet, solemn, and even more confidential. He was getting to what he really wanted to say. "Ricky Scalise got taught a lesson too. Only no one ain't gonna find him piled up anywhere."

Stunned, Peter sat back. He looked from one to the other, Joey was nodding his head, little, short, sad shakes. Barbie looked away, out the window to the coagulated street. For a moment, Peter couldn't make the leap from the news of the dead Dobermans to this information. Joey's timing had given no greater significance to one over the other. As comprehension sunk in, he at least understood the reason for the somber mood he had detected when he came in. It had to be for more than a mountain of dead dogs.

Joey's voice was barely audible. "Word is, he was gonna tap the till. Real big. Then take off. You don't do that, Peter."

What Peter had known of Ricky Scalise, he had liked. The man had been quick-witted and funny, but Peter never realized the depth of his involvement. He had known him only on the same casual basis that he knew maybe a dozen or so other characters who moved in the gray area between the legal and the illicit, who were involved with varying intensity in the underworld structure of the metropolitan area. And his acquaintance was strictly the result of being a regular at Sam's. He chided himself for his naïveté in romanticizing these people. This news shattered little-boy stereotypes of folksy heart-of-gold characters beneath tough exteriors.

"You know," Joey said, "you live around here, you don't screw up, they take care of you. But, boy, you do screw up, things happen fast."

Peter put in a decent interval of finishing his coffee. He had no more appetite for the second cup he usually got or for the colorful anecdotes he loved at Sam's. He couldn't drive the image of Ricky Scalise from his mind, a guy, he guessed, he hadn't really known well at all, a guy he'd never see again.

He got up, nodded goodbye to Joey and Barbie, and forced himself to think of something else as he walked back to the Jaguar.

But the only other thing he could think of was a pile of fifteen dead dogs and that wasn't much more pleasant.

Peter drove back to his apartment in a somber mood. Alison Bradley's disappearance had been festering in his mind, especially since the night he and Nancy had dinner with Doug Symonds. At first, as a defense mechanism against the unacceptable, he refused to entertain any sinister explanation. But the alternative, that Alison had simply pulled up stakes, didn't make sense. He knew Alison and Doug too well to believe that.

Now this story about Ricky Scalise. Obviously, the man had been playing in a rough league and his demise was an occupational hazard, but, insofar as their casual relationship allowed it, Peter felt a real loss.

But he told himself that he would not dwell on that which he couldn't control. He would read the *Globe*, have an hour's run along the Charles, shower, lunch at Jake Wirth's, and spend the afternoon at the Boston Public Library. The evening was a bright glow to end the day: theater at the Music Hall with Nancy and dinner afterward at Maison Robert. He fastened his mind to the thought as he drove and his mood lifted.

He parked on the street. As he was walking to his apartment, his *Globe* tucked under one arm, he heard his name hailed. Mrs. Beauchesne, who lived two doors up and around the corner, was striding with purpose toward him, Andrew, her black Scotty, tethered to her arm. Andrew apparently found Peter's sidewalk just right for his deposits, which, fortunately, had a pellet-like consistency and could easily be nudged with a stick into the street. Mrs. Beauchesne was not wont to use a scooper, and Peter, liking the old lady, did not wish to make an issue. So often under cover of darkness, he'd make a sweep, purging the brick sidewalk with a piece of stick.

"Peter!" Mrs. Beauchesne came up to Peter. She seemed agitated. Her pudgy, short body was well protected from the chill air by an expensive coat and hat that to Peter looked as if they were from some species probably exotic and endangered, maybe lynx. Andrew was protected by a black-and-white-checked coat that buttoned under his belly.

"Oh, Peter, it's dreadful. I'm so upset." Peter regarded her while Andrew sniffed his feet. More bad news, no doubt, but probably not too macabre, Peter hoped, not another dark cloud.

"I suppose I'm lucky, actually. They didn't hurt Andrew and the little dear must have raised a fuss. If I'd been home, they wouldn't have hesitated doing God-knows-what to a defenseless old lady."

Peter thought he detected a note of wishful thinking in her voice.

"There, there." He put his hand on her shoulder. "Now, tell me what happened."

"Last night. While I was out, they broke in." Mrs. Beauchesne clutched her chest, jerking the leash and Andrew's head back. Her wattles quivered with emotion. Andrew regarded her with wary eyes.

"Who—"

"Oh, I don't know who. Those drug addicts, I suppose. Oh, God. But they knew what to look for. I'll say that much for them."

"Oh, that's terrible, what—"

"I was home at eight o'clock. I had come straight from bridge at Lucy Thompson's. I knew right away that something was wrong when I got inside from the way that Andrew was behaving. I think that it was quite a shock to him. He's very sensitive, you know. He can't take disruption of any sort. The little man is set in his ways."

"I've noticed."

"Naturally, the police have come, although God knows what they're capable of." Mrs. Beauchesne relaxed the grip on her chest, and Andrew, taking advantage of the slack on the leash, resumed his olfactory examination of Peter's cuff, intrigued by traces of Clark.

"Whoever it was came in through my bedroom window."
Mrs. Beauchesne rolled her eyes at the words as if their mere
mention hinted at scandal. "They got jewelry—I won't tell you
what it was worth, except plenty. They got my china—Royal
Doulton, I'll have you know—and they got my silver. All of it."

The old lady's eyes watered and she plucked a lacy handkerchief from her purse and dabbed behind bejeweled specta-
cles. Andrew backed up quickly to avert whiplash.

Peter wasn't surprised at the story. Breaking and entering,
like mugging, drugs, vandalism, and various perversions, had
invaded Beacon Hill, long a bastion of Boston culture and respectability. Mrs. Beauchesne, while not exactly a Brahmin,
was virtually a relic, a hanger-on.

"Well, now, I wouldn't be at all surprised if the police had
some luck," Peter lied. "It sounds as though everything must
be very identifiable."

"Oh, what good will that do? They'll melt down the silver, I
imagine, pull apart the jewelry, sell the china for one-tenth of
what it's worth and still get plenty. Can't you just see the kind
of table it'll be set on?" She shuddered.

"I don't know, Peter, what I'll do. I've lived here all my life.
I love this neighborhood but it's not like the old days. It's not
safe anymore, inside your home or on the streets at night."

Andrew tugged on his leash. He had wrung all the information from Peter's cuff that he cared to.

"You're a man," she continued, pulling back the straining
Scotty, "and you'll get by here just fine. Of course, they can
break into your apartment but at least you're safe on the
street."

Andrew tugged again, whined, and looked up at his mistress. His body quivered beneath his checked coat.

"Maybe I should get one of those German shepherds or
Doberman pinschers." Peter thought of fifteen dead Dobermans. "Andrew's a darling, but he'd frighten off absolutely no
one."

Maybe you could throw his pellets at them, Peter thought
uncharitably.

"Well, Mrs. Beauchesne, I'm very sorry about what happened. But as you say, at least you weren't hurt. Or Andrew." Peter hated expressing that sentiment, one of the absurdities of the times: that one should be grateful that only one's belongings had been violated.

"Oh, I know. I'm grateful for that." With difficulty, she bent down to the dog and scratched his head. "I'm grateful, aren't I, Andy, yes, I am, yes, I am."

Andrew wiggled in ecstasy as Mrs. Beauchesne scratched and babbled a stream of baby talk at him.

Taking that as a cue, Peter expressed his regrets again, opened the wrought-iron gate, and went to his front door.

He caught a glimpse of Andrew lifting his leg against the front Michelin on the Jaguar as he went inside.

CHAPTER 5

"Why so glum?"

"Who's glum?"

"Who's glum? You. You're glum."

"It shows, huh?" Peter Swann said. He reached across to the ice bucket for the Mâcon Chardonnay.

"A little bit. You didn't do much more than grunt at appropriate intervals during the show."

"That's not so," Peter said, refilling his and Nancy's wineglasses. "I don't grunt. My responses to anything are invariably highly informed, articulate commentary."

"Ha." Nancy Brewer sipped her wine and toyed with her coquille St. Jacques. She looked pert and elfin with her curly dark hair and deep brown eyes. "Perhaps 'glum' isn't the word. 'Preoccupied' would be *le mot juste.*"

Peter sipped and toyed in return.

"What did you do today?" she asked.

"I ran this morning."

"How very unusual. Don't tell me. Along the Charles, I bet, just to be different. No one runs along the Charles."

"Nancy, you are a master, or should I say a mistress, of irony."

"A what?" She laughed, showing white, even teeth. "I suppose there's a good comeback there but the wine has dulled my wit."

"And made you even more reticent than usual. You could have said there are worse things to be mistress of."

"That's not a very good line."

"I suppose not."

Nancy sipped some more. "Okay, so you and ten thousand other trendy bastards in search of longevity, tranquillity, oneness with God, nature, self, and whatever, ran by the Charles. Then, let me see, Locke-Ober's? Cricket?"

"Running has passed the trendy stage. It's a fact of life. And I had lunch at Jake Wirth's."

She made a small gesture with her hand that said: Okay, I should have included that in the list.

"Then the BPL." They said it together and then laughed.

"I'm that predictable, huh?"

"Just a bit. You've become a creature of habit. What you need instead of the library is some world travel with a suitable companion. Like me."

"There's no frigate like a book."

"English teacher. Okay, so far nothing in the schedule to throw you into a funk. Unless you're tiring of leisure, suffering puritanical guilt feelings at lack of productivity."

"Not yet."

"Your running time was off then, or maybe it's an attack of shin splints or Achilles tendonitis."

"No. I ran an excellent time for just training. Eight miles in fifty-five minutes and fourteen seconds."

"Impressive." She lit a 100-millimeter cigarette. "I can't crack fifty-five minutes myself."

Peter ignored the taunt and refused to comment on the cigarette. Although Nancy wasn't a heavy smoker, her smoking was a thing with them. And she refused to run.

"Well, then, let's see, that leaves tonight. I hope it's not the company you're keeping."

Peter touched her hand. "Hardly. Actually, it's really not much of anything. Wait, I take that back. It isn't trivial. It's that business with Alison. That's mainly it, but . . . then this morning a couple other things happened." He told her about Ricky Scalise and Mrs. Beauchesne.

Inhaling on her cigarette, she regarded him. "It's too bad, but you admit that Ricky was virtually a criminal."

"He was a nice guy."

"I'm sure." She shrugged. "And Mrs. Beauchesne. That's too bad too, but that kind of thing happens all the time and she *wasn't* hurt. Besides, she's loaded."

"So what? It was traumatic for her."

"Of course it was, but, Peter, think of all the poor people in the world whose daily lives are trauma. I mean all the time."

"That's irrelevant and you know it. Christ, we'll be getting into philosophy on the relative conditions of mankind in a minute. I'm simply relating to people that I know."

They toyed with their food, finished their wine, and assured their inquiring waiter that everything had been, indeed, just fine. He seemed genuinely pleased at that but just a trifle distressed when they declined the dessert menu.

"We'll go to my place," Nancy said. "I'll treat you to a real gourmet dessert."

Peter double-parked near Quincy Market and ran into Swensen's for two banana splits.

"I'll run this off but I don't know where you put it," he said, regarding her petite, slender body as he got back into the Jaguar with the two banana splits.

"I've probably burned off two thousand calories just shivering in this thing. Let's not eat them here. I'll hold them while you get us back to my toasty apartment."

"Real homey," Peter said. "What's it like living in a phallic symbol?"

"Warm at least, my love, which is more than we can say for this James Bond fantasy object. Can't you build a fireplace in it? You could use the dashboard for wood."

"Love me, love my car."

Peter drove past the Aquarium and pulled into the parking area under Harbor Towers. They took the elevator thirty-six floors to Nancy's apartment.

"There," she said, settling on the sofa, feet curled under her, "isn't this nice?" She attacked her banana split. "Mnnn, this beats those fancy French desserts by a mile, doesn't it? Lots cheaper too. Never let it be said I'm after your money. I'm just an old-fashioned girl who loves the simple pleasures."

Peter grunted.

"You're grunting again."

Peter swallowed. "Dammit, I had a mouth full of ice cream, pineapple, nuts, and bananas. Besides, your question was rhetorical."

"Actually, Peter, I've been thinking of Alison too, a lot." She knew how the situation was bothering Peter and had tried to keep the tone of the evening light.

Peter swallowed and held his breath a moment. He was eating the ice cream too fast and the cold had stabbed his sinuses. He finally said, "Bad as it is, I wanted to believe that Alison just took off. But I can't. It's totally out of character."

"Which leaves?"

"Which leaves something not very nice, I'm afraid."

"Poor Alison."

"Yeah, and poor Doug."

They ate in silence a few moments. When she had finished, Nancy said, "Want a beer?" Deliberately, she made her tone light.

"It doesn't exactly follow ice cream, but yes."

"I'm going to have a little amaretto. Rather have that?"

"Beer's fine."

Nancy turned on a soft rock station on the stereo system and went to the kitchenette. She brought back a Beck's dark for Peter and amaretto on the rocks for herself.

"Let's look out the window." She wanted to lift the mood.

Thirty-six stories below spread the waterfront park. To the left, Government Center and part of the business district high rise loomed, the jumbled shapes checkered randomly with lights.

"Isn't this pretty? You've got to admit that this beats the view from your place."

Peter bent forward, pressing his head against the glass, and peered straight down. "Handy if you're into suicide. It's got my place beat for that, although I guess one could impale himself on my wrought-iron fence. But it wouldn't be as quick and you wouldn't have the fun of the free fall," he said.

She laughed, happy at what she took for his improved spirits. She linked her arm through his and rested her head on his shoulder. Paul Simon crooned in the background.

"You know what, Nance?"

"What?"

"I think I'm going to look into this."

"Into what? The comparative suicide accessibility of our apartments?"

"No. Into Alison's disappearance."

Nancy took her arm from Peter's. "You're kidding. You're going to play detective?" She felt her own mood start to slide.

"No-o-o. I don't know how to do that. But God knows, I've got time. Look at it as an existential exercise. I mean, the police are busy and, let's face it, they're confronted with this type of thing all the time. They have no personal interest in Alison, they don't know that she wouldn't just take off. There's no sign of foul play, so they go with the obvious conclusion."

Nancy led him to the sofa. She knew she couldn't fight his preoccupation with Alison's disappearance but would try to have him keep some perspective.

Peter sipped his Beck's. Its astringent taste had driven out the sweetness of the banana split. "Well, I think first I'll go to the police. See what they have."

"Now, you be careful. I don't think the police are going to be particularly thrilled with any meddling."

"I'm not meddling. A citizen has the right to make inquiries."

"Maybe you ought to get yourself a trench coat. You know, to go with the Jaguar."

"Very funny." He knew her joking was well-intended.

"I mean, a down vest and stocking cap just don't cut it."

He ignored her teasing.

"I think I'll also check out the cemetery where she ran."

"What do you expect to find there?"

"I don't know. There's been no trace of her car. You know, there are two ponds there. I don't know how deep they are."

She caught her breath slightly as she got his meaning. "Oh, God, Peter, you don't think . . ."

"Every once in a while you read about that sort of thing. Someone going off the road into a river or lake or something and not being found for a couple of years."

"Don't you think the police would have checked that out?"

"I don't know. I'll try to find out."

He sipped again. She sipped.

"I'll be careful, I'll be discreet. I don't want Doug to find out that I'm looking into this."

"Of course not."

She rested her head on his chest and stroked the hair at his neck. "Just make sure you are careful. And now, my budding Boston Blackie, I'm a working girl and I need my beauty rest. Computers are unimaginative but they do demand that their keepers have an alert mind."

"I detect a subtle hint."

"But not for you to leave. Unless you can't stand a night away from your beloved brick sidewalks and murky gas lamps."

"When the alternative includes you, my princess, I can put up with the shallowness of chrome-and-plastic high rise."

"Let's get with it, then," she said, getting up and leading him into the bedroom. There was more than one way to lift a man's spirits.

Lieutenant Arthur Gabriel leaned across his desk, smoke from the Pall Mall dangling on his lip curling into his eye, and assessed Peter carefully. And, Peter felt, just a tad contemptuously. The cigarette's a good touch, Peter thought. Richard Widmark or Sinatra.

"So, Mr. Swann, you think we've been sitting around here doing nothing, that we don't know which end is up?"

"No, I think you're on top of it," Peter said. "But as I explained, I knew this girl, I know her fiancé, and I'm just a concerned citizen expressing that concern. Just letting you guys know that there's someone out there who cares, that's all."

Lieutenant Gabriel squinted through the smoke, the Pall Mall jittering in his mouth as he spoke. "I can appreciate that, Mr. Swann, but if you'd look at what the facts are, I think you'd agree that at this point there isn't much else to do."

Lieutenant Gabriel leaned back, adjusting his thin buttocks on the blown-out cushion of his swivel chair. He took the Pall Mall from his mouth and rested it in the notch of a black plastic ashtray whose contents spilled over onto his desk.

"Point," he said, "the girl disappears, last known headed for Oak Way Cemetery. No trace, nothing, of the girl or her car. Those two ponds you mentioned. You know, we're not all that dull. The thought occurred to us too, so we checked them out. Went all around them. The banks are muddy all around both and the ground wasn't frozen all that much, so that for a car to go in, there'd have to be a sign. There was no sign."

Lieutenant Gabriel went for the Pall Mall as though he'd been a long time away from it. He sucked deeply on it and the smoke twirled from his mouth and nostrils as he spoke. "Unless some creature in the pond reached out and grabbed the car. You don't believe in monsters, do you, Mr. Swann?"

"I didn't, Lieutenant, but then I was skeptical about police efficiency, remember, and you are just demolishing that skepticism."

"Point," Lieutenant Gabriel continued, "we questioned the people in the cemetery—the workers, that is—and they have not seen the girl or her car.

"Point. We have put out a missing person's bulletin. It's been out maybe two weeks. Nothing on it. No sign of girl or car.

"Point. Despite what you say about this girl not being the type to pull a 'see ya later' on her boyfriend, her job, her friends, you are seeing this from your perspective, and no offense, but it's limited. You just haven't encountered this kind of thing before. We do. All the time. And often the people left behind are shocked. Can't understand it. Like you."

Peter sat back in the old wooden chair he had pulled beside Lieutenant Gabriel's desk when he was ushered into the little cubicle that served as an office. The office looked like something from a TV series: memos and bulletins on a board; desk top disheveled with paperwork; bottled-water cooler in one corner.

He regarded Lieutenant Gabriel. Skinny, mid-forties, hair combed to one side, slicked with hair tonic. The man was a wise-ass, cynical, almost stereotyped. Probably worked at it, though. Yet Peter sensed an efficiency, a canniness that he hadn't been willing to concede when he came into the station.

Nancy had been right. The police were rather standoffish about his queries, rather guarded at what they saw as implied criticism. Peter had said nothing about doing any digging around himself. It was obvious what the reaction to that would be.

"So that's it, then? In effect, there's nothing more to do? I mean, what about her fiancé? What's he do, just sit around?"

Lieutenant Gabriel shrugged. He looked tired. He snuffed the Pall Mall out in the crowded ashtray. "There's no body. So far there's been no crime that we are aware of. She wasn't a juvenile. She wasn't running away from debts. She has the right to take off."

Lieutenant Gabriel leaned back again. "Look, Mr. Swann, I don't mean to appear unsympathetic, but for my money, this Bradley girl will show up soon. She had some kind of pressure, some problem, she needed to think it out. It's *not* unusual."

Peter stood up. "Lieutenant Gabriel, thank you for your time. Probably you're right," Peter said, not wanting to be argumentative.

"That's what we're here for, Mr. Swann."

Outside, Peter sat in the Jaguar watching his breath plumes as he assessed the situation. This was the point where on TV or in books the private detective would be called in. The police had gone as far as they could on what was available and were too busy to keep digging around a case that they did not see as sinister.

Maybe, just maybe, Gabriel was right about Alison going

off to get her head on straight. It would be nice if it were true but Peter knew he didn't believe it.

Peter now considered that his plan to go to the cemetery was pointless. The police had checked it out. The possibility of Alison having accidentally driven into one of the ponds had bothered him, but that appeared eliminated.

Where would a TV detective go from here? He didn't know. He blew a long stream of breath at the walnut dashboard, clouding the speedometer and tach, and drove home.

CHAPTER 6

Tommy Stella watched the neon sign flash L-I-Q-U-O-R-S. A long, lighted arrow slashed through the "Q" and bent in toward the door to the liquor store. Tommy was across the street from it in the doorway of a closed appliance store. Bad place to hang out, he knew, especially after dark. Cops go by, they'll hassle me for sure, he thought. Probably pick me up. Maybe that's what I want. Naw, no way. Screw them. Don't want nothing from the cops.

Tommy lit another joint. He had just finished one a few minutes ago and one not long before that. But they weren't calming him the way they usually did. Nothing had been able to calm him since that late afternoon, what was it, just a few days ago? Seemed like weeks.

He shook his head and sucked deeply on the joint to drive the image of what he had seen from his mind. Tommy was a tough kid from a big-city neighborhood and was used to some grim scenes but never anything like that. It wasn't popping wheelies on a Beeza 750 to see a guy get his brains blown out. Jesus.

And he fell like a sack of the potatoes Tommy used to lug from the storage room to the bins out front. Nothing like the way it was on some of those old TV reruns where the guy checking out might drop to one knee and fall with dignity. BAM and down he went, twitching a few times before they lugged him off. Christ, they didn't even give him a chance to say any last words.

That had been enough for Tommy. Talk about hauling ass, that old Charger could still fly. But, oh mother, had they seen me? he wondered. Tommy was pretty sure they had but not good enough to know who he was. Something would have happened by now if they knew.

Tommy scrunched his wiry neck into his jacket collar, threw away the joint even though it still had plenty of life in it, and put his hands in his pockets. Despite the cold, his jacket, black leather, was half open at the front. Regulations. Likewise, his shirt was open at the throat, exposing the almost translucent, white skin. Geez, almost eighteen and only about three chest hairs.

Where the hell was Frankie? Tommy didn't have a watch but he guessed he'd been waiting a half hour. When he left the house, he had just told Frankie he'd meet him by the liquor store in twenty minutes. Frankie would use his wheels tonight, a pretty nice van. Tommy had kept the Charger in the driveway since *that* afternoon. It was too easily spotted and he didn't want to be seen in it. He had a vision of being forced off the road and gunned down, his body jerking up and down like a rag doll, à la Bonnie and Clyde.

They would pick up some brew, blow some weed, maybe get a couple of chicks. But most important, he'd tell Frankie about that afternoon. He hadn't told anyone yet, at least not the particulars, although he had told Frankie that he'd seen Mr. Scalise buy the farm.

He shouldn't have followed the Caddy. He should have minded his own business. But when those two guys came into the store, there wasn't much doubt about what they were. Shit, they might as well have worn signs. Those guys had seen too many showings of *The Godfather,* Tommy thought.

They hadn't seen him or Frankie. They had been crouched down loading produce under a counter an aisle over from where those two goons strolled right down the middle of the store into the back room where Mr. Scalise was.

When they didn't come right back out, he and Frankie ran to the side window and saw them lead Mr. Scalise out the back door to the Caddy. Was there some rule that said you had to use a Caddy for that kind of stuff?

He told Frankie that he was going to follow the Caddy, see where they were taking Mr. Scalise. Frankie had said he was crazy, that he'd just get himself into trouble. He should have listened.

But he had had to follow. Mr. Scalise was an all-right guy, didn't really hassle them and paid more than minimum wage. Not that he had been any use to Mr. Scalise.

Course, he and Frankie had been out of a job since that day. It was real funny the way that had worked out. The store simply didn't reopen. Mr. Scalise used to open it in the morning and a couple of old retired guys would run it until he and Frankie came in after school. The store was never very busy. He often wondered how Mr. Scalise had made a buck at it. Now he knew. He didn't. The store had just been a front.

Anyway, the store didn't reopen. Simple as that. No sign on the door, Due to Death of Owner, that kind of thing. The cops didn't come sniffing around. Nothing from Mr. Scalise's old lady. Nothing. Mr. Scalise was just gone. Poof. And no one knew how, where, or why except the guys who did it. And . . .

Tommy shivered. Where the hell was Frankie?

Time for another J. He unsnapped his jacket pocket and took out a joint from the metal Band-Aid box. His hands were goddam cold.

He had to fill Frankie in. Had to tell someone the whole thing or it was going to drive him nuts. His mother had been on his ass about what was wrong lately but that was nothing new. Far as she's concerned, something's always wrong.

And school. Couldn't stand that bullshit even when things were smooth but now couldn't escape the dumb questions by sleeping. Too nervous.

Tommy backed deeper into the doorway and pulled on the joint, holding the smoke in his lungs. He looked across at the package store and let the smoke out in a long stream when he saw the Cadillac. Was it the same one? Looked like it. Black, '80, '81. He couldn't make out who was in it or whether they had spotted him. He cupped the joint in his hand and tried to withdraw into himself.

The driver got out and then another guy. Tommy felt his knees go weak. They were the same ones. No mistaking the big one. They started toward the liquor store, and then just after a car went by, they were charging straight across the street at him.

Tommy didn't recognize the animal yowl that came from his throat. He was running up the street but it was like those dreams he had had as a little kid. You were running but not going anywhere, and the monster was close behind.

He turned into an alley and right away saw the high fence at the end. Stupid. He turned around, knocked over a barrel, and sprang back out of the alley. The two guys were less than twenty feet away.

Tommy ran. His lungs were already searing and his side felt as if he had a knife in it. Goddam pot and cigarettes. Why hadn't he joined the track team like the jocks and fags? He expected any minute to feel a bullet zip through his head and pictured *his* brains flying out in front of him, a grayish-reddish paste.

Where the hell was Frankie? Where the hell were the cops?

Ahead was an intersection and a main drag. Gotta make it to that. Should be help there. Lots of people. They wouldn't dare do anything with lots of witnesses around. They were afraid of witnesses. That's why they were after him.

Ignoring his tormented lungs, Tommy put on a burst of speed and turned right at the intersection. The main drag was brightly lighted with lots of traffic. Just ahead a short ways was one of those big discount drugstores that sells everything but cars. Still flying, Tommy turned for a quick look. They were gone.

"Aw right-t-t-t!"

He ducked into the drugstore and skittered over to the magazine and book counter against the wall where he could watch the door. He tried to control his breathing as he bobbed his head around to assess the layout. Was there a back door? There had to be. One of them could come in that way and the other through the front and trap him.

Probably shouldn't have come in here. Naw, he was safe. Too many people around. But couldn't stay here forever. That was the problem: getting out. They would be waiting. He could probably outrun them but those bastards wouldn't mind plugging him right on the street like a dog.

On the other side of the store were the public phones. He'd call Frankie. Maybe he was still home. Have old Frank pull up out front with the engine running and they'd be off. The van had a 350 in it and could move pretty good, although that Caddy didn't look slow.

He moved toward the phones and nearly tripped over a couple of little kids ogling some toys wrapped in plastic and cardboard hanging from a pegboard. He glanced down at them and, looking around, started toward the phones again. Two more aisles.

At the phones, he fished in his pockets. No change; he'd have to break a five. He'd go to the register down front where he could see a chick working rather than go up back where the pharmacist was. Those guys always acted like they were in pain and this one would probably get pissed if you asked him to break a five.

Better go to the back, though. Too easily spotted from the street by that front register. Could buy some aspirin or something to keep the starched-up old pharmacist happy.

Tommy started toward the back and didn't see the huge man step around the aisle until he had him by the arm. "Keep your mouth shut, kid, or I'll spill your brains right here. I shit you not, I'll do it."

Tommy felt himself go boneless and a huge rushing sound filled his ears. The store swam as the big man led him down the aisle by the arm past the pretty girl at the cash register and outside into the back seat of the black Cadillac.

They drove for about twenty minutes, and when they

stopped and the big man pushed him outside, Tommy recognized instantly where he was.

He said, "Mama," once before everything went black.

Harold Parkins knew he was going to be sick, just like after the time with that pretty young girl. Oh, had he been sick that night, spilling out the whiskey, burning him as it came up, spouting from his mouth, trickling freely from his nostrils. It had come up until there was nothing left except the spasms that wracked him for a long time afterward as he sat in his own stink and filth in an alley a short way from Eddie's bar.

Finally, he had dragged himself to his room, where he lived alone, and managed to make it to the sanctuary of his bed, where he lay for a long time trying to stop the image of that pretty young face from crowding his head and threatening to explode his skull. The face rippled as though it were underwater, as though it were melting, smiling at him, but the flesh, the lips melted, and the smile became a horrible accusing leer of long teeth and the face became a skull because the face wasn't underwater, it was . . . it was burning.

This time, though, it hadn't been a pretty young woman but almost as bad. This one was just a kid. Strip off the veneer of juvenile tough and he was still just a boy, too young to have done anything to deserve this.

But at least he was already dead, although obviously hadn't been for more than five or ten minutes. He had been still limber and warm and the blood had still been flowing but was down to a trickle.

And the boy had been the work of *them*, not of Alex or anyone in his crew, in Harold's crew. That should have made it a lot better, but it didn't; it didn't make it any better, because the boy was so young.

Harold had done what he was supposed to, what he *had* to do because he was afraid to do otherwise. He was in too deep. If he balked, he could very easily go the same route as all those he had sent on their way. His expertise wasn't so special that he couldn't end up in the oven.

He thought he might be sick while he was doing this job, but he wasn't. He contained himself until he had finished and was on his way home. This time, though, he didn't stop at Eddie's. The whiskey had only made things worse the last time.

Before he got home, he stopped by the Fenway and made it into some bushes before he exploded. He stayed there for several minutes on all fours, trying to keep the boy's face from smothering him.

But the boy's face became the young woman's face and then they intertwined and he couldn't tell which was which.

CHAPTER 7

"It's a waste," Joey Blowtorch said, low, almost into his coffee. "A goddarn waste. Matter of fact, I don't believe it."

Barbie Melons bobbed her head vigorously in agreement. She clutched her coffee in both hands and peered into it as if trying to find a meaning.

Peter stirred sugar and raised a quizzical eyebrow. He had just joined them. A cold, thin rain scattered on the window, thrown by tight gusts blowing in from the northeast. A two- or three-degree drop and it would be snow.

Joey leaned back and examined the day outside the window. "Weather sucks. You know, I never used to mind the winters until the last couple of years. Must be getting old."

"Move to Florida," Peter said.

With his finger, Joey traced a squiggly design in the steam on the window and then wiped it away and peered out. The rain sounded like flung sand.

"That's turning to sleet. I'll be glad to go home and hit the sack. Goddarn house is freezing, though. Can't even afford to stay warm."

Joey turned from the window and took a swallow from his cup. He bit from a powdery white doughnut that sat, a half "O," on his napkin. "I don't know about Florida, Peter. I couldn't take that trailer-camp life. Shuffleboard and bingo, that's not for me. Besides, the summers are hot as hell. I move, it'll be to Arizona or someplace out West."

"I got a cousin in Arizona," Barbie said. "I visited her a couple of times. It's real nice out there, Joey. You'd like it."

They nursed their coffees. Joey bit at his doughnut again

and Barbie finished a canoli. Peter wondered how you could start the day with a canoli. He watched an exchange of money at the counter. Sam wrote something on a pad of paper.

"So what's a waste?" he asked. "You said something was a waste."

Joey looked at him. "Nothing. I was talking, that's all. Around here is a waste, I guess you could say."

"You ever think of shifting jobs to the Chamber of Commerce?"

"I ain't in no mood for jokes, Peter." Joey finished his doughnut and stood up. "You want a doughnut or something?"

Even though he didn't really want one, Peter found himself fishing in his pocket. "Yeah, get me a plain doughnut, Joey."

Joey waved him away. "It's on me. Some morning I want bacon and eggs, you can buy. Barbie, you want another canoli?"

Barbie nodded. "Sure. Why not."

Joey pushed to the counter.

"Lots of calories in one of those, Barbie," Peter said. "How many do you figure?"

"I don't know. I don't count anymore. I've got a lot of upkeep here, you know?"

Peter smiled. "So what's bothering him?"

"Aw, just something. He'll be okay when he gets some shuteye. I never could figure out how someone could work nights. I mean, he's been nights at the GE for almost ten years. Since he went straight." She laughed. "He was nights before that too, I guess, but that was different. He made his own hours then."

Peter smiled as he thought of Joey's former skills that had earned him his sobriquet and some time as a guest of the state.

"Got you another coffee too," Joey said, balancing three coffees, and doughnuts and a canoli wrapped in napkins.

When he had sat down, Peter said, "Coffee doesn't keep you up, Joey?"

"Not like this, with the booze. The way you drink it, straight, might keep the old mind a-whirling. But two or three of these"—he lifted his cup—"and sitting around here to bullshit for a while and I can knock right off soon's I get home."

Joey broke off a piece of doughnut and dipped it in his coffee. For a few moments they were busy with their doughnuts, canoli, and coffee. Finally, working a paste of doughnut and coffee from his gums with his tongue, Joey leaned back and looked out the window. The rain, half sleet, was a steady, driven spray.

"Where you parked, Peter?"

"Right outside."

"You finish your coffee, you can give me a lift? I'll get soaked."

"Sure. You want a lift anywhere, Barbie?"

"Thanks, but I'm going to stick around here for a while." Peter wondered whether she was going to have another canoli.

He finished his coffee and he and Joey nodded and slapped their way to the door, then skipped across Hanover Street through a logjam of traffic to the Jaguar.

Peter drove slowly through the crawl of Hanover. The defroster howled futilely and Peter enlarged the puny cleared spots with a cloth. He turned right into a street not much wider than an alley that overleaned with tenements, neat stacks of brick and wood, kept up, not run-down or sordid. He stopped in front of a brick four-decker, terraced with porches, a colony of several families, mostly related.

"You know, Peter, I like this neighborhood. Clean and safe. And friendly. Everyone knows everyone. Not like in the suburbs where you don't know the people three houses down even though they've been there for twenty years."

Joey stretched his feet as if looking for nonexistent warmth from the heater. "I got a good thing going now, Peter. Wish I had settled into it all along. I like working jet engines. It's a challenge, know what I mean?"

Peter nodded.

"GE's a good place to work. Good dough, good bennies. I like it. I like working nights too." Joey looked at Peter. "You're the guy with the sweet deal, Peter. The state does numbers, it's okay. We do it, it's a crime. Where's the sense to that?"

"I'm lucky, I guess."

"Damn right you are. When I think how I used to screw around, get in trouble. No percentage in it. Now I keep my nose clean, maybe a little numbers, stuff like that. Nothing more. Cops don't mind that 'cause no one gets hurt. It's the other stuff that'll get the cops on you."

Peter shut the defroster fan off and wiped the windshield with the rag. Joey lowered his voice as if the world outside the Jaguar were listening. "Remember I told you about Ricky Scalise a few days ago? Now get this, this really sucks. Kid that worked for Ricky got it a couple of nights ago."

"Cops?"

"Naw, not the cops." He glanced at Peter, his tongue excavating more doughtnut from under his lips and gums.

Peter made an expression that said: Why?

Joey shrugged. "I'll tell you this much. Everyone's real pissed. The kid wasn't from around here—he was from Chelsea, name was Tommy Stella—but he's got relatives here. No one big, though. I don't think you know them. Point is, you don't touch a kid. I'm surprised they did."

"What did they do to him?"

"Don't know for sure. Took him for a ride and hasn't been seen since."

"Jesus."

"Paulie Deleo's brother seen the kid getting hauled off. Followed part of the way, then screwed." Joey looked absently at the rain beading and pathing the windshield a moment. "Don't blab this around, huh? I mean, everyone knows but I wouldn't go flapping my gums about it. I'm telling you 'cause I'm pissed and I've known you a long time, Peter."

"What about the Deleo kid? Will they grab him?"

"I doubt it. I think they know everyone's pissed and they'll probably try to cool it. See if it just blows over. I'm sure the kid knows enough not to go talking to the wrong people."

"Where did they take this Stella kid?"

Joey swallowed something. "Like I say, I don't know. Paulie's brother followed them as far as Oak Way Avenue before he turned around. Know where that is, Peter, up by that big old cemetery?"

"It *was* very good pizza," Nancy said.

"I'd nudge it into the excellent category, maybe even outstanding."

"I think the parameters of judgment break down in those upper ranges."

"Wow, have you ever got your jargon down pat. What you computer types do to language."

"Come on, you know me for a warm, loving, highly complex person. Not at all a technicrat." Nancy pushed her seat all the way back and stretched out. "As a matter of fact, I'd cuddle right now except that this traveling icebox of yours, in addition to being sans heater, doesn't allow it. A stick shift has come between us. See what you give up for having this oneness between man and machine?"

"What do I give up?"

"Oh, I would be fondling your curly blond locks, nibbling at your earlobe, whispering provocative things, promises of what's to come."

The headlights of the Jaguar probed the twists and turns of Route 127, a rambling, scenic drive along Boston's North Shore. The morning's rain had turned to a cold mist. Peter felt a disquiet that he hadn't yet broached to Nancy. And she hadn't asked yet about his inquiries into Alison's disappearance. He knew she thought it was simply foolish meddling on his part and she wasn't going to feed any nascent fires by displaying curiosity.

After his conversation with Lieutenant Gabriel, Peter had been willing to drop the matter and hope for the best, but what Joey had told him this morning seemed to imply a link between Alison and . . . Peter wasn't sure what.

"Nance, I want to bounce some probabilities at you."

"About what?"

"Remember when I told you about Ricky Scalise?"

"The mob guy who was dipping into the till and got himself vaporized?"

Peter made a face at the word "mob," but let it pass. "Right. Well, this morning when I was at Sam's, the guy who told me about that laid this on me. The kid who worked for Ricky at his store has apparently disappeared."

"What do you mean, 'disappeared'?"

"I mean he was taken for a ride."

"How old was he?"

"I don't know. High school kid, I guess."

Nancy pulled herself up in her seat. "These are nice people you associate with."

"I don't associate with them. Anyway, the community is just a trifle upset. I guess we have a violation of code here, hitting someone that young."

"We're talking about people who deep down are really warm and sensitive."

Peter ignored her sarcasm. "The point is, obviously he saw something he wasn't supposed to. I'm not condoning any of this, just relating it."

Nancy turned off the radio, which had been straining to hold an FM station. "You know, Peter, I don't think it's very smart of you to hang around that place. I know you find it interesting and I know that all kinds of ordinary people, city workers, even cops, use it for a watering hole and for scuttlebutt, but it seems to me that they tell you things you might be better off not knowing."

"Like what?"

"Like what? Like knowing that Ricky whatever was rubbed out. I mean, it didn't even make the papers. Sounds rather secretive, don't you think?"

"No. That was common knowledge. It was meant to be

known as a lesson to others. It didn't make the papers because no body was found."

"Well, like this kid, then. I suppose that didn't make the papers either."

"I don't know if it did or will, but even that is common knowledge in the community. Although, as I say, they're pissed about it."

Nancy hunkered back into her seat and hugged her arms across her chest for warmth. "That's what I mean. Common knowledge within the *community*, whatever the definition of that is. But you are making yourself included in that group and I don't think that it is a good idea."

"Look, Nancy, I've been in and out of the North End for years. Since I was a kid. I've told you that. Had a cousin who lived there I used to visit. I got to know a lot of the people. I've known this Joey guy for I don't know how long."

"And now that you've got the time, you go every day."

"There's nothing wrong with that. When anyone thinks of Italians they immediately think of the Mafia, for godsakes."

"Well?"

"Look, most of these people are plain, ordinary, decent people. But it's a relatively small, close-knit community, so they know who's involved, what's going on. I admit, many of them are involved in minor stuff like the numbers but that doesn't mean they all go running around with machine guns."

They rode in silence for a few minutes. They were traveling through Beverly Farms now. The moon had temporarily broken through the clouds and was glinting coldly off the gray Atlantic to their left.

Nancy broke the silence. "Well, anyway, you mentioned something about probabilities."

He looked at her. Although he was miffed at her reaction and had decided to say no more, her eyes, large, brown, and intelligent, broke his small resistance. They always did.

"Okay," he said, "it seems that this kid's friend was supposed to meet him last night but was late. As he was coming up the street, he sees his buddy getting chased by two muscle types."

"Muscle types?"

"Yeah, leg breakers, hit men." He paused and looked directly at her. "Killers. They do what they're told to do, paid to do."

"Oh," Nancy said in a small voice.

"So this kid, whose older brother knows the guy who told me, sees these two goons chasing his buddy. He follows at a distance. To make a long story short, they catch the kid and drive off with him. Oh, by the way, both these kids worked for Ricky, and the goons are the ones who took Ricky wherever, the kid is pretty sure. They saw Ricky being taken away."

"The plot thickens."

"Wait a minute. He follows just so far and then gets scared and turns around."

"I still don't get what you want to know about probabilities."

"Just this. Joey says that when this kid turned around, he was on Oak Way Avenue, that he followed them that far."

"So?"

"About the only thing Oak Way Avenue leads to is Oak Way Cemetery. I mean, you probably wouldn't use it unless you were going to the cemetery. If you were going to wherever else it leads to, you could take a shorter route."

Nancy stared at him. "Wow. But wait a minute, that doesn't have to mean a thing. I mean, it couldn't. Alison wasn't connected with . . . with crooks and killers."

"I didn't say she was. Joey certainly doesn't know anything about her. He just mentioned Oak Way as by-the-way information. When he did, I really pumped him. But discreetly."

"Do you think the fact that this kid was on Oak Way is common knowledge?"

"I don't know. Joey didn't seem to attach any particular significance to it. It was just part of the narrative. Like I said, they're upset and I think there could be some real reaction but that's neither here nor there as far as we are concerned."

Peter touched the brakes and downshifted to second at a sharp bend in the narrow road. The ocean had been replaced by large estates fronted by rolling lawns and high fences of concrete columns and iron spikes.

"What I'm getting at is, here I am, a disinterested third party who in a matter of a relatively few days hears first about a girl who goes jogging at a particular location and disappears, and second hears of a teenage boy with no known connection to jogging girl, but who is a witness, I guess, to a probable crime, being taken for a last ride to presumably the place where the girl disappeared. What are the odds of a connection?"

"Oh, gosh, Peter, I don't know."

"There's this to consider too: the man for whom the boy worked has also disappeared. Same place?"

"Course, you don't know for sure that this kid was taken to the cemetery."

"No, but it's a good bet. Assume he was. What are those probabilities?"

"Peter, this isn't the kind of thing that I work with. Your guess is as good as mine."

"My guess is that there is a connection."

"That's because you want there to be one. You feel very badly about Alison and are looking for something to go on. What did the police say the other day when you went? I presume you went."

"Yes, I did. They thought Alison took off and would be back soon. At least the guy I talked with thought that."

"See."

Peter turned the radio back on. He didn't want to talk about it anymore. Nancy wasn't even making a good sounding board. Or maybe she was, he conceded. Maybe he felt she wasn't simply because she wasn't confirming his opinions.

"Want me to get a station?"

"Yes. Something soothing."

"Oh, we're getting touchy." She slid across and half sat on

the transmission hump. One hand searched for a station while the other brushed his neck.

"Peter, now don't take this as a criticism. Trust this to be an objective analysis. You have been fed some random information which superficially connects. You are terribly concerned about Alison and even about this Ricky guy. I also think that because you have a great deal of spare time and want something to occupy you, you are forcing connections. You are looking for a puzzle."

"That's absurd," he snapped. "I don't regard this as a game."

She looked fondly at his strong profile, the planes of his face, and knew she should back off a bit. She snuggled in close. "I didn't know you had Italian in you."

"My mother was one-quarter Italian." He put his hand on her knee. "Watch out, because that means I have a sinister side, you know. You haven't really seen the Peter Swann of stilettos and secret, Old World-type oaths and codes."

She laughed. "Look, why don't we stop someplace, buy ourselves a game of Clue, go to your place, or mine, and work out these urges you have to be Simon Templar or Philip Marlowe."

"Or Spenser." He grinned at her.

"Or Spenser." She kissed his ear. "Watch the road," she purred. "Or even better, we *don't* pick up a game of Clue and still go to your place or mine."

"I like that better." He downshifted to third and spurted past an old pickup truck wallowing over the road.

Ahead, a sign said TO ROUTE 128. He'd take that to Route 1 and be in Boston in less than a half hour.

CHAPTER 8

The next morning, Peter skipped coffee at Sam's. The rain had stopped but it hadn't cleared and the forecast was for snow in the afternoon. He had things to check out and was anxious to start.

But first a run. It was a real departure from routine to run before he had had a light breakfast to raise his blood sugar and had a chance to walk out early-morning muscle stiffness. Today, however, would be an exception and he knew he'd be glad when he finished that he had done it.

So, dressed in inexpensive gray sweats, expensive gray-and-maroon New Balance running shoes, woolen cap and mittens, Peter pumped his way, more slowly than usual, along by the Charles maintaining a 7:30 pace by checking his Casio chronograph against points previously calculated.

The light wind at his back was cold, the river a fish-belly gray, and the tops of the John Hancock and Prudential buildings were amputated by the low ceiling. Peter nodded and waved to the parade of other runners who, as always, struck him as a set-up showcase of Boston's intellectual and business community.

It took him three miles to achieve the easy and fluid rhythm that he usually hit almost right away, the point of ease where the body took over, a running team of heart, lungs, and legs throbbing their smooth power.

He ran another mile and turned around into the wind. The whiffs of catalytic-converter rotten eggs, diesel musk, and city background noises were the only real intrusions. He remembered Doug telling him once that was why he ran in the cemetery. It was quiet and the air was sweet. Peter planned to try it one day soon. And not just for the quiet and the air.

Back home, he showered, fed Clark, had a light breakfast of cold cereal, juice, and coffee, and dutifully skimmed the *Globe*. He then looked up the address of Ricky Scalise's store in Chelsea. That would be his starting point. Next, he found three Deleos in Chelsea and wrote down the addresses.

He was still somewhat miffed at Nancy's suggesting last night that he found this an interesting riddle. Her attitude puzzled him. She knew how he felt about Alison and Doug. His feelings toward Alison were platonic, yet Nancy acted almost jealous, he thought.

Dressed warmly against the mid-twenties temperature, he headed for Chelsea on the Tobin Bridge. He liked to think of the bridge by its original name, the Mystic River Bridge. It had, he thought, a better ring to it. Good names shouldn't be squandered.

He took the off ramp to Chelsea and quickly found himself in a maze typical of the street tangle of Greater Boston, a labyrinth of former cow paths and conflicting signs.

With time and luck, he finally found Ricky's store on a long main drag. He pulled over and paused across from it. Closed tight. Nothing to be gleaned here, although Peter didn't know what he had expected to find. The store was probably filled with rotting produce and not even the grace of black crepe or his picture in the window. As if he had never existed. What the hell, Peter thought, it's almost 1984. Ask anyone in the neighborhood about Ricky Scalise, and they'd probably give the old Orphan Annie eyes and say, "Who?"

He checked the addresses of the three Deleos on his note pad and crisscrossed an area of four blocks before giving up and looking for a place to ask directions. He couldn't find a cop or a taxi and settled for a package store. It was a couple of minutes after nine and this one must have just opened. It was a wonder the winos weren't lined up outside, he thought, for the neighborhood didn't exactly suggest gentlemen in town cars stopping by for Harvey's Bristol Cream for M'lady.

He parked directly in front. The package store, old, long, and narrow inside, was dimly lighted, and the proprietor, short, stocky, in his fifties, eyed Peter curiously. Eddie Bauer down vests and Pendletons didn't usually drop in, especially at 9 A.M.

"Yezzir?"

"Morning. Would you know whether any of these streets are located nearby?" Peter read the three streets.

The man gave a little motion that said: It figures, just directions. "Yeah, Hayward's two streets over, parallel with this."

Peter wondered how he had missed it. "Actually, I'm looking for a kid. High school age. If he wasn't in school or at home, you got any idea where he might hang out?" As he said it, Peter felt that the question was stupid, but, after all, this was on-the-job training.

"Depends on the kid. What's his name?"

"That's not important."

The proprietor was gazing past Peter toward the door. He scratched over his right ear at coarse silver hair, releasing little flecks that swirled lazily toward the counter.

"You a cop?"

"No."

"Private cop?"

"No."

"Come on, you're a private cop, right?"

"Honest. I'm not."

The man pulled a pipe from his pocket and packed it. Peter was surprised at the pipe. You can never tell, he thought. This guy had cigar written all over him. Unfiltered cigarette at least.

"I don't think I can help you," the man said, his fingers moving from pouch to pipe.

Peter turned to go. "Thank you, anyway," he said.

"Wait a minute. Most kids around here hang out at Bunky's. Next street over, take a right. It's about three blocks down. Can't miss it. Pool, pinball, all those electronic games. You know the kind I mean? Jesus, enough to give you a friggin' headache. I mean, I can see a nice quiet game of pool or billiards, but these kids today gotta be dazzled with all kinds of light and noise."

The man held a lighted match over the bowl of his pipe and sucked rapidly a few times. The flame dipped up and down. The smoke was aromatic.

"You know how I can tell you're a private cop?"

Peter went along. "No. How?"

The proprietor pointed the stem of his pipe at Peter. "Number one, your clothes. A regular cop might go for the outdoors look like that. I mean, today they hardly ever wear the old-style stuff, you know, suits and ties. Some of the old-timers do. Although, actually, I wouldn't be surprised to see that come back."

He sucked five times in rapid succession. "Anyway, your stuff is quality. Too expensive for a regular cop. I got a good eye for clothes. I'm right, huh? That's good stuff."

Peter smiled.

"First I thought you might be a pusher but you ain't the type. I mean, a guy comes in asking around for a kid, you gotta wonder. I see a lot of people and I can usually tell about 'em. I figure you're legit. Besides, a pusher's not gonna go around asking questions in public. He'd know where the kids are."

For a moment, the man regarded Peter through his smoke as though waiting for a confirmation of his analysis. Peter started to thank him again but was interrupted.

"But the clincher's your car," he said, nodding toward the Jaguar. Peter obliged by turning to look.

"What kind is it?"

"Jaguar."

The man came from behind the counter and led Peter to the doorway, where he looked out at the Jaguar. "Nice-looking car. She runs nice?"

"On the whole. Actually, it's rather old."

The man nodded and puffed a moment. "Me, I say buy American. No offense. You guys got an image and I can understand that. Gimme an Olds or a Buick any day, although they ain't what they used to be. My nephew's got one of them British cars. What the hell is it, M.G.? I guess that's it. College boy. Gotta have the little foreign convertible."

"As you said: image."

"Yeah. But it's a pain in the ass. She won't start half the time. If it's too cold, too hot, too wet, too cloudy, you name it. I mean, I'm exaggerating, but you get the picture. She's fussy as hell." He puffed three times. "Yours like that?"

"You mean temperamental?"

"Yeah."

"Sometimes. But I think I know what your nephew's problem is."

"Yeah? What?"

"He's got a female. You said 'she.' They had a lot of trouble with the female M.G.'s. Males run great, but the females can be real bitches."

The man looked at Peter evenly. He blew a puff of smoke. "That's very funny," he said.

"Yeah, well, thanks for the directions. Bunky's, huh? Next street over, take a right, three blocks down."

"You got it. Hey, wait a minute." The man walked back to the counter. "Here." He tossed Peter a nip from a basket by the cash register. Four Roses. "My compliments. It's cold out."

"Thanks," Peter said, pocketing it. Did this guy know about the Jag's heater?

Peter drove to the pool hall–pinball machine hive. A sign said Bunky's Entertainment Center. Real subliminal hype. He stopped in front and looked through the large plate-glass windows. Four pinballs and electronic games were being worked and two games of pool were in progress. It was a big place. Peter counted three rows of four tables each and a slew of games around the walls.

He was surprised at the way the guy in the package store had suddenly opened up to him. It was like the old axiom that if you acted the part or did something as though you should be doing it, most people would accept it.

So now he had a place to look for the Deleo kid, but he didn't know what he looked like and chided himself for that. The fictional detectives would know, would have a picture at least—or would they? There had to be a starting point. He told himself he was being too self-critical in assuming that he should be at some point further along.

From what he could see, those inside Bunky's looked older than high school age. But judging a kid's age by looks, especially at a distance through a window, was, he knew, tenuous. When he had taught, the physical maturity of many high school juniors and seniors had surprised him. Based on looks alone, they could easily pass for drinking buddies.

Should he go in and—and do what? He didn't know how to approach this. There was no way out but to make inquiries. That was bound to raise eyebrows, asking about a person who had worked for a man and been friendly with a kid each of whom had been eliminated.

What could he say? He had no badge, no authority. He couldn't assume everyone would be duped like the guy in the package store.

Maybe he should just forget the whole thing. This really was none of his business. He was meddling, actually, in a way, committing a breach of confidence with Joey.

But then he thought of Alison again. And Doug. At this point, there was no way he could just forget the whole thing.

The inside of Bunky's Entertainment Center instantly depressed Peter. The incense of cigarette smoke was part of the fabric of the place, garnished with suggestions of pot and sweat. A cue ball clacked off a three ball, which clacked off a seven ball, which clunked into a corner pocket. Tough angle, nice shot. The shooter, who tried to resemble Fonzie and succeeded, eyed Peter curiously, then concentrated on the table. A tall, rugged kid, who looked to be in his early twenties but with a gut already well on its way, had his soul poured into an electronic game. On its screen, spaceships zoomed and veered toward him, but he was staving them off with a death ray that whooshed like a gas-station grease gun. *Victory at Sea*, 2044. Organized mindlessness to inaugurate the day. Now Peter knew why he liked the Boston Public Library in the morning.

At the back wall was a counter and Peter went to it. Packs of peanut-butter crackers and machines for cigarettes and Coke ensured that no one's nutritional needs would ever be wanting in Bunky's. A man sat behind the counter, reading a magazine with the cover folded back. Bunky himself? Peter wondered.

Peter stood at the counter a moment before the man looked up. "Wanna table?" He took in the down vest and the Pendleton.

"No, thanks. I'm looking for a kid who might hang out here sometimes."

"Yeah?"

"Maybe you know him and could tell me when he's likely to come by."

"Maybe."

"Name's Deleo. I don't know his first name."

The man deadpanned Peter a moment, then stood up. He had about three inches on Peter. "Who wants to know?"

"I do."

The man pushed his cheek out with his tongue and made a sucking noise. "You a cop?"

"No." Déjà vu, Peter thought.

"Are you the goddam truant officer or something?"

"No." Would the private-eye question be next?

"Well, then, who the hell are you?"

"Look, I just want to talk to this kid, that's all. I hear he might come in here once in a while. It's no big deal. He's not in trouble."

"What do you want to talk to him about?"

"That's between him and me."

"Yeah, well, I suggest you get your ass out of here. You want to play pool, I'll give you a table. But that don't look like your style. You sure you ain't supposed to be out hunting ducks and got yourself lost?"

Peter deadpanned in return for a moment but it didn't produce any satisfactory effect. Finally, he said, "Sorry to bother you. I'll let you get back to your *Intellectual Digest*." It wasn't a great comeback but the man's antagonism had surprised him.

The whoosh of the death ray goosed his ears as he went back to his car.

The man behind the counter watched Peter walk back past the row of tables and, when he went outside, got up quickly and went to the front window. He took in the registration number on the Jaguar and, repeating it to himself, went back to the counter and wrote it down. Then he went into another room and used the phone.

Peter drove back by the package store and then two streets over to 721 Hayward, the address of the Deleo closest to Ricky's store. He stopped in front. It was about what he expected. Triple-decker on an old street in a tough neighborhood of multi-unit dwellings and small businesses.

Now what? What was he going to ask this kid anyway? And why would the kid have any reason to talk to him, to answer any questions? Peter sat and thought of his options at the moment. The kid was either in school or had skipped school and was out at the old fishing hole like Huck Finn. Probably the best time to find him was in the evening.

Maybe he'd come back out and nose around some more before picking up Nancy at eight. Maybe he wouldn't. For now, he wanted a cup of coffee and to use his bathroom.

CHAPTER 9

At five-thirty, Peter was back out. It had been dark about an hour and the snow had just started to fall. The latest forecast said it would continue into the next morning, with several inches likely.

Peter planned to go back to Bunky's Entertainment Center, wait outside, ask around, and see if he could find the Deleo kid. He'd see whether the kid would tell him anything about why Tommy Stella had disappeared. If he couldn't find Deleo or if he wouldn't open up, which Peter admitted was extremely likely, then he would drop the matter. End of budding career in detection. He would settle into a life of contemplation and introspection. In any event, he promised himself he'd be back at his apartment by seven-thirty in time for a shower before meeting Nancy.

The closest spot to Bunky's he could find was around the corner and down a block. It was a dim street, slimy with the sheen of snow that hadn't yet fortified itself into whiteness against the traces of road salt left over from a previous dusting. He didn't like leaving the Jaguar where it was so susceptible to vandalism, but he wouldn't be long.

Peter couldn't see the force propelling him into the darkened alley. A vise had him around the waist and was lifting him off the ground, his feet kicking the air helplessly. "What the hell—"

His face slammed into the bricks and he heard something crack. White pain seared across his cheek and he knew he was bleeding. The vise released him and he fell to the ground. Although he couldn't focus clearly, he knew he was looking at

CEMETERIES ARE FOR DYING

specks of broken glass on the asphalt. He tried to get up, but the ground, the specks of broken glass, were spinning beneath him.

"Get up, you mother—"

Something slammed into his buttock, tipping him over so that his back jammed into the brick wall. Eyes still refusing to focus, Peter looked up at his tormentor.

"Son of a bitch. I said get up."

A booted foot sprang at him. Peter brought his knee up to protect his stomach. The boot cracked off his knee and caught him in the upper chest and throat, forcing the wind from him and ramming his head into the bricks again. He could hear deep racking coughs and was surprised to discover that he was making them.

The vise, smelling of stale sweat and leather, lifted him into a standing position. "When I tell you to get up, you get up. You understand?"

Without being aware of the process of descent, Peter discovered that he was sitting. He saw denim-covered knees in front of him and knew that one of them was preparing to strike his chin. His elbow absorbed much of the blow but still his head bounced back into the bricks again and for a brief moment he was able to ward off passing out before he fell to his side.

He must have been out for several minutes, for when he looked around, whoever had assaulted him was gone. Opposite him, maybe ten feet away, was a dark blue van. His eyes were still not focusing well and the light in the alley was very dim. A burly, almost fat figure strode toward Peter.

"Hey, man, you okay? You had us worried for a while. Thought you checked out on us," he said, looking down, one boot toe pressed into Peter's stomach.

Peter's face and head felt swollen and hurt as though he had had massive doses of Novocain whose anesthetic properties had worn off. His throat was constricted and he didn't think he'd be able to talk. Cautiously, he ran his fingers through the hair on the back of his head. It was sticky and warm. The boot pressed further into his stomach. Nausea welled within and he spilled bile over the boot.

"You bastard." Peter heard laughter from the van as the boy—boy? man? Peter wasn't sure—rubbed the smeared boot on Peter's down vest and under his chin. He was surprised that he wasn't kicked again.

"Hey, Danny," a voice called from the van, "the guy was just trying to shine your boots." Peter saw the laughing figures come from the van. They stood around him.

"Make him do the other boot," someone said. They all laughed but Danny.

Peter guessed there were nine or ten of them and he saw at least three girls. They stood in a semicircle, grinning down at him. Several had beer bottles in their hands and some were smoking. He could smell pot.

He tried to clear his head and assess his situation. He was sitting in an alley surrounded by—he forced himself to count—nine figures in the uniform of youth. They looked a couple of years out of high school. Across the wide alley was the van. Parked about ten feet to his right under a fire-escape ladder was a beat-up sedan. Cardboard boxes of trash were piled near the sedan against the building. On the asphalt, speckles of broken bottles glittered in the faint light thrown in by a streetlamp mostly obscured by one of the buildings at the corner of the alley.

Peter didn't know whether he was seriously injured or not. Certainly for the moment he was in no condition to run or resist. He was groggy and weak. The side of his face and the back of his head hurt where he had been slammed into the wall behind him. His left ankle somehow had been twisted and was stabbing him. He felt his best strategy was to let them have their way for now until he regained some strength unless it appeared that he had no choice but to fight.

Pulling his down vest tightly under his chin, he began to shiver. It was cold and the snow was steady but light. He could feel his watch on his wrist and his wallet against his buttock. The significance of not having been robbed suddenly struck him.

"Hey, I think the man's cold. Hey, man, you cold or something?"

Peter heard giggles. He looked up but didn't know who had asked the question. Two tall, strong-looking boys stepped forward, grinning. Lifting Peter under his arms, they pulled him up and supported him against the building. The grins widened and they winked at one another as they stared at him, their faces inches from his.

"Hey," said one, "you stink like puke."

"Let's wipe that puke that's drippin' down your chin, man," said the other. "It'll freeze if we don't. What we got to wipe that puke off with? Let's see." He opened Peter's down vest and pulled his Pendleton loose. With a sudden motion, he ripped the shirt up the front.

"Hey, that'll sew right back, man. Don't worry." They all laughed. The boy spilled some beer onto the piece of torn shirt and jammed it into Peter's face, rubbing viciously back and forth. As Peter felt his legs start to go, the boys held him up. "That took care of it. Your face is clean now, man."

"How about a drink?" said the other. "Here, have some beer." He jammed the bottle into Peter's teeth and tilted it upward. The beer ran out of his mouth, down his chin, and onto his torn shirt.

"Hey, don't you like our beer? It ain't polite not to take a drink when it's offered you."

"Maybe the man's too cold to take a drink just yet," Danny said. "That's probably what it is. He's too cold. He'll have a drink with us after he's warmed up. Won't you, man?"

As Peter attempted to button his vest, his cold, stiff fingers refusing to function, Danny said, "You guys help him, huh? Can't you see the man is trying to button up?"

"Keep your hands off me," Peter rasped. His throat ached from the blow and seemed to be closing on him, but he was determined that if they touched him he would damage as many as he could before they subdued him.

The two pulled back in mock hurt and the figures behind them giggled appreciatively. "Geez, we're just trying to help," said the one who had poured beer onto him.

Fingers fumbling, he felt like a fool trying to button his vest as they watched.

"Think he'll finish tonight?" asked a voice from the group.

"Don't you worry about this guy," Danny said. "He'll see it through. He's a real big man." They all laughed and Peter felt shame crowd in with his fear and pain. He considered pushing this to a climax now but again decided to wait. As he finally pushed the last button through its hole, the figures all clapped their hands in applause.

"That's better, but I bet you're still cold," Danny said. "What can we do to warm you up? You got any ideas?" Danny scratched his head reflectively. Peter heard the others giggle in anticipation of a show. "Hey, I know. How'd you like to make it with one of the girls here?"

The group hooted and whistled at the suggestion.

"Yeah, we can all go into the van and you can do it there," Danny said. "We've got some stuff that'll make you feel great too. Man, you never had it the way you'll get it from these chicks."

Turning to the group, he said, "Girls, c'mere, so the man can see you." The girls stepped forward, smiling at Peter. They seemed younger than the boys—still in high school, Peter thought. Jesus. He felt nauseated again.

"This here is Joanne, Vicky, and Betty. Take your pick. They're all good and don't worry about hurting the others' feelings. Maybe you can make it with all of them." Danny reached over and tapped Peter gently on the chin. "Come on, man, pick one, for chrissakes." He looked back and forth from Peter to the girls. "I like Vicky—hi, honey."

The girl stepped forward and rubbed against Danny. She smilingly appraised Peter.

"Hey, you're gonna try and make it with one of these chicks, ain't you? I mean, it wouldn't be good manners not to.

Might make them feel bad. I asked you a question. Are you gonna try? . . .

"I think you'll try," Danny said with a short laugh when Peter didn't answer. "If you don't, I'll waste you right here and now." His tone was flat.

"Waste him now," said a voice. The group edged forward.

After a moment's indecision, Danny said, "No, we'll let him go out in style."

He came in close to Peter, pressing a leather-gloved finger into Peter's chest. "Which is more than you deserve, pal. I hear you're a nosy bastard, asking questions, looking for people that don't concern you."

When Danny backed away, Peter slowly let himself to the ground. He needed to get off his ankle and he thought it might not be bad strategy to appear resigned and submissive until the time when he would sell himself as dearly as he could.

Danny looked down at Peter with contempt. "That's right. You rest your ass." He turned to the figures behind him. "Jerry, get down to the front of the alley and watch out for the cops. The rest of you get in the van and fix up the seats so there's room. I'll stay here and make sure our friend don't go away."

For a few moments, Peter and Danny held a staring contest until struggling and cursing and voices from the van turned Danny's head. "Jesus, Danny, how the hell do you move this seat? Give us a hand, huh?"

Danny looked down at Peter, mumbled something, and walked to the van. Peter forced himself to think. He couldn't yell for help. He couldn't run; he felt he could barely crawl. But he had to do something quickly. Danny was in the van and would soon have the seats arranged.

He felt as though he was going to pass out but forced himself to concentrate. He glanced up and toward his right at the fire escape. Normally, he thought, he'd be able to get to it before they could stop him. But where would it take him? Still, it would have been a chance. Anyway, the beat-up sedan was in the way. He'd have to go around it.

He stared at the car, rear end toward him. Could he lock himself in it? Even if he got to it in time, he was sure they could break their way in. It might even be locked now. He wondered whose it was. Apparently it wasn't abandoned, as it had a current rear license plate.

Gaze fixed on that license plate, he barely dared to hope. He knew it was his only good chance and he would have to take it now. Cautiously, he felt in his pants pocket for the book of matches that he carried for Nancy. Usually carried. It was several seconds before he could find them and he was sure this was going to be the classic perverse situation of not being able to find something you usually had at the time you needed it most.

He looked at the van. They were still busy inside and were paying no attention to him. He opened the book. Only one match left. He felt a brief anger and frustration but quickly quelled them. This was to be a bluff for which he'd need only one match.

Slowly, he began to edge toward the car. The pain in his head and face was intense and he felt as though he was going to cough with the effort of sidling on his rear. He paused, holding his breath, and looked at the van. They still hadn't observed him. He had moved about four feet and still had another six feet to go. He felt a slight pressure in his right hand and saw a piece of brown glass sticking from the fleshy pad below the thumb. The lack of pain made him realize that his hands were anesthetized from the cold. He pulled the glass sliver out—it was a full quarter inch. To his surprise it did not immediately bleed. He stared at it fascinated.

He began to sidle to his right again, using his right hand to support his weight as he shifted toward the car. He expected at any moment to hear a leering voice challenge his progress. He was almost there. Another shift and he was leaning against the bumper.

Incredibly, they still hadn't noticed him. He pulled the

matchbook from his pocket and ripped the remaining match out. Then he pulled at the license plate and it snapped down. Holding it down with his right forearm, he reached over with his left hand and unscrewed the gas cap.

"What the hell's he doing!" Danny screamed, bursting from the van toward Peter as the others stared stupidly.

"Don't come any closer," Peter said, throat burning as he held up the match, "or I'll splatter you all over this alley."

Danny hesitated.

"I—mean—it," Peter said deliberately. "If you come any closer, I'll throw this match in the gas tank."

Danny stood maybe ten feet from Peter, the snow, heavier now, swirling around him. "You're bluffing. I think you're full of shit, man."

"Try me."

Danny took a step forward. "No way you're going to blow yourself up."

Peter put the match to the cover of the book.

Rocking back and forth on his heels, Danny glared at Peter. His eyes blinked rapidly in indecision.

Sensing Danny's vacillation, Peter decided to take the offensive. "If I throw this match in now, you're too close to get away. I figure I've got nothing to lose." The two stared at one another for a moment. "Now, you're making me nervous, so I want you to start moving back." Merely talking tortured Peter's throat.

"Hey, man, we weren't going to hurt you. Honest. We was just kidding."

"Move!" Peter said, putting as much force into the word as he could.

"He's bluffing, Danny," said a voice from the van.

Danny looked over his shoulder. "I notice all you brave bastards are behind the van. Come up here with me if you think he won't."

With the match touching the striking surface of the cover, Peter moved them to within an inch of the open gas-tank nozzle. "Move back now or you're going to be part of the bricks in about two seconds." Despite the seriousness of the situation Peter almost laughed at the melodrama of the words. Did they sound as corny to Danny as they did to himself?

Peter thought that perhaps they did when after a few moments Danny didn't begin his retreat. When his hands began to shake involuntarily from the cold, Danny said, "Okay, okay, I'll move back, but I'm going to watch you freeze on that bumper, you bastard."

With relief came a consciousness again of the pain in his head, face, throat, and ankle. The numbness in his hands made him wonder whether, if he wanted to, he could strike the match or, if successful in that, he could, without fumbling, put it into the gas nozzle. More than that, would gasoline explode in the cold, if indeed the tank wasn't empty? Moot questions, since he had no intention to self-destruct. He'd go down swinging first, pitiful as that attempt might be.

Very carefully, he put his left hand with match and matchbook under his vest. Still holding the license plate down with his right forearm, he blew on his hand for a moment and then leaned back on the trunk of the car.

They were all in the van now except for Jerry maintaining his vigil at the end of the alley. They were quiet and watchful, looking out intently at him. The glow of cigarettes or joints made him imagine the warmth inside the van and he began to shiver again.

Then he began to feel drowsy and his eyes started to cross the way they did when he had had too much to drink. He longed to nod off and then wake up with everything all right. As the temptation to sleep became overwhelming, he thought of the stories of people trapped in the snow and cold and how sleep was actually their worst enemy. Worried about his head, he feared lapsing into a coma. Mostly, he knew he must stay awake to fend off the wolf pack ready to tear him apart. Intrigued with the analogy, he became aware of another sensation. He had to urinate. The feeling was making him shiver even more. As he thought of it, the urge became intense and he considered relieving himself as he sat there but knew that holding it would help keep him awake.

The van's engine coughed into life and Peter could smell its exhaust. Danny's head emerged from the driver's window. "Hey, man, how you doing? Getting cold? You should come in here. It's nice and warm and the girls are still waiting."

The head stayed outside the window and Peter knew that Danny was checking to see whether he was still awake. So that he wouldn't come close to investigate, Peter croaked, "I'm just fine."

The head withdrew but shortly an arm flashed out the window and Peter caught the glint of a bottle as it arced toward him, shattering as it struck the bumper beside him. As he instinctively covered his face with his right arm, the license plate snapped shut. But he wasn't cut and he quickly pulled the plate back down.

They were out of the van now, lined up and throwing at him. Hunching his head down but keeping his gaze on them, he protected his face with his left arm while he held the match and book closed to the gas-tank nozzle. Bottles exploded off the trunk and glass struck the back of his head. A bottle struck his left elbow as he raised it to protect his head. Abruptly, they stopped. He wheezed as he breathed rapidly with the exertion of his concentration.

"Find some bricks or something," Danny was ordering.

Peter fought the panic that was beginning to well up. He knew he'd never be able to withstand a barrage of bricks or rocks. He coughed and his throat and head hurt incredibly. His right hand was bleeding again from the puncture of the glass sliver.

Suddenly, an agitated Jerry was running up the alley, and the others, urged by the whispered curses of Danny, clambered into the van. Peter watched them pull from the alley and turn left on the street. As they swung out, the flash of the blue revolving light in their windows filled him with pure elation.

The van and the cruiser had pulled beyond the end of the

alley. Blue light pulsed off the wall and the scratch of the police radio was softened by the snowy air. Peter attempted to yell but his voice perversely refused to rise above a deep, hoarse whisper. Breathing in deeply and using all his strength and concentration, he willed his voice to scream. It was louder but he knew they couldn't hear from the street.

Surely, they would be coming in to investigate. He knew they would. It was illogical that they wouldn't check the alley from which the van had come. Then he would be saved and would taste retribution.

The pulsation of blue on the alley wall suddenly stopped and Peter could hear the van pull away. He listened intently. He could still hear the cruiser's engine and radio. Apparently they were satisfied and wouldn't be coming into the alley after all, he thought. He could picture them writing a report in their car and knew that they would be leaving at any time.

He tried to rise but his legs buckled and he fell back against the bumper. He had to get out before the police left or he might not be able to get back to the car before the van returned. And he was sure it would return.

Putting the match and matchbook into his pocket, he began crawling toward the alley entrance. Something in his head seemed ready to explode and he wondered whether he was having a stroke. He heard the police radio crackle again. They must have their door or window open, he thought. He wondered how long it took them to do a report.

He could scarcely breathe from the exertion of crawling and knew he'd never make it to the street. Certain that his throat was going to close on him, he spat horrible-tasting stuff onto the asphalt.

He had to get their attention. He summoned all his strength and dragged himself to the cardboard boxes of trash. Tipping one over, he crumpled a piece of spilled newspaper into a ball and reached back into his pocket for the match and matchbook. For a moment, he fumbled with benumbed fingers and couldn't find the match. Finally, he pulled them out and rested on one elbow, his breath rattling in his throat. He listened. He could still hear the cruiser's engine. He blew on his hands and flexed his fingers as rapidly as he could. If the match went out . . . He grasped it as tightly as he could between his thumb and forefinger and placed it on the sandpaper. For a second, he gazed idly at the congealing blood at the base of his thumb. He rubbed the match against the matchbook. Nothing. He rubbed again. The head of the match was wearing out against the abrasive surface as they do when wet. He must have gotten blood on it. Again he rubbed and with a small puff the match flickered weakly. Shaking as he attempted to shield it, he placed it against the newspaper. He coughed and his head began to swim.

CHAPTER 10

"You *are* crazy, you know that, don't you?" Nancy Brewer said, getting up to go to the kitchen.

"Ah, that's what I like in a woman, tender words of endearment." Peter was stretched out on his favorite chair and ottoman by a fire of oak and hickory logs. "Oh, my princess, while you're up, would you get me a Grant's?"

"A what?"

"Nothing. Just get me a frosty flagon of nut-brown ale, please."

Nancy returned with two Labatt's beers and coiled on the floor beside Peter's chair.

"There's a good wench." He took his bottle, patted her head, and lazed back reflectively in his chair, enjoying the fire and the faint whistle of a sharp breeze outside. It was early evening but he was already drowsy.

"You know, you would be better off if you had never won that money. You would be busily and gainfully employed, waging, like the rest of us, a minor struggle against adversity instead of trying to fill your time acting like Sir Launfal rescuing damsels and slaying dragons."

"You interrupted me. I was just about to say something profound on the condition of mankind and my own humble efforts to improve it."

She pulled her head away from his hand. "You're lucky you weren't killed. Or permanently maimed. Or frozen to death."

"That's redundant."

"What is?"

"Frozen to death and getting killed. And you forgot to

mention perhaps being burned to death. That trash was going pretty good when the cops found me. But seriously, Nance, before my encounter of the worst kind with those Neander-thals, I had just about decided to give up. You know, ac-knowledge that I had no business nosing around and probably couldn't find anything anyway."

"You were right."

"Maybe, but—"

"Oh, damn, don't tell me that you've seen some kind of sign or message in the fact that you survived, that you're destined to see this through."

Peter sipped from his Labatt's and studied the green bottle a moment. Softly, in the background, over the FM stereo, Bar-bra sang, sweet as a lute. "No, no. Nothing corny like that. It's hard to verbalize what I mean."

"You're the English major."

"Well, it's just that it would be awfully easy to do nothing. Look, I'm not trying to be a Hemingway hero, but I'll admit I am finding some satisfaction in at least attempting to help Doug put some sense to Alison's disappearance. Not knowing has got to be real tough on him." He looked at her evenly. "On me too, I admit. And I'd like to see it through as far as I can until I come to a point where I can honestly say I just don't know what else to do."

"And you're not there yet."

"No. I'd still like to talk to the Deleo kid. He saw things that might be important."

"You're still insisting on a connection between that Ricky guy and Alison."

"Not insisting. Suggesting."

Nancy sipped from her beer and began to peel the label with a long manicured nail. "Well, I still say you're crazy to go back out to that neighborhood. You spent a night and a day in the hospital and have been home for only a week."

"Nothing broken, although I'll admit to some surprise at that. I thought for sure I'd broken a cheekbone or had a hairline fracture in the noggin. Spare me the corny jokes on that, if you please. As for the rest of it, just bruises and a hurt ego." Peter wondered if that wasn't the real reason for going back out, to prove something. "Besides, there is no connection between what happened in the alley and what I'm trying to find out," he lied.

"Says you. For my money, you were getting an unsubtle suggestion to butt out."

Peter made a noise of dismissal.

"When do you plan to go out there?"

"When I finish this beer."

Peter pulled the Jaguar to the side of the street and prepared to make a U-turn.

"Just what are you doing?"

"I'm taking you back."

"Oh, no, you're not. We went all through this. I can be just as stubborn as you. If you insist on going back out into the jungle, then I insist on being by your side. You Tarzan, me Jane. Besides, you said there was no big deal to this."

"There isn't."

"Well?"

"Okay, okay." Peter popped the clutch and headed toward the Tobin Bridge and Chelsea.

"Anyway, I plan to wait in the car," Nancy said. "Speaking of which, by the way, either I am going to have to invest in a down sleeping bag for this rolling Amana, or you do something about the heater."

"Yeah, yeah, tomorrow."

"Sure, sure."

When they got to Chelsea, Peter double-parked four car lengths from the front of Bunky's Entertainment Center.

"Actually, I guess it's just as well you came along. This way I can park in front."

"What do you plan to do?"

"Wait by the door till someone comes along and ask them if they know where Deleo is."

"Clever strategy."

"What do *you* suggest?"

"Why don't you just go inside and ask?"

"Bunky didn't take a shine to me."

"Maybe you should think of running for ward councillor around here. You seem to really relate to the folks."

Peter got out of the car. "I'll go take up position."

"Should I leave the engine running for a quick getaway? I mean, it wouldn't be for the heat."

Peter scrunched down into the collar of his pea coat and waited a doorway down from Bunky's. His head and cheek were still tender from his beating but not too badly and his ankle felt nearly normal.

It had been a close call, no doubt about it. Was he pushing it a bit, tempting fate? Was he simply wasting time? Was there a god of foolish human behavior who alternately clutched his sides and pointed to him as his finest accomplishment?

After about five minutes, he wondered how long it would be until someone went into Bunky's. He was dressed warmly but already was beginning to feel the chill of twenty-two damp degrees. He could wait in the car with Nancy, but anyone dropped off would easily be in Bunky's before he could get to them.

No, he'd have to wait where he was. He shifted back and forth on his feet, which, despite insulated boots, were becoming cold. Grace under pressure.

He heard them before he saw them. High-school-age males. He recognized the type immediately. Slightly junior editions of his friends in the van. The high school he had taught in had had its share. Leather jackets open at the front, despite the cold. But collars up. The gait, actually a swagger, slightly bandy-legged. Peter was reminded of documentaries where the male of the species exhibited plumage or horns or teeth to warn other males and entice the females. This tight-clothed strut was a human counterpart. Did they practice it? When he had taught, he noticed that the wholesome kids, the ones with the books and calculators, or those in the band or chorus, never had the walk. Just the hard guys.

Peter stepped out to intercept them before they went into Bunky's. "Hey, guys, wait a minute, will you?"

They stopped and eyed him evenly, smiling little mirthless smiles at each other. He watched them carefully as he approached.

"You guys know a kid named Deleo?"

The smiles vanished and the hardness went soft.

One stared at the other, who gaped at Peter a moment and then bolted back in the direction he had come.

The boy had the advantage of youth, a litheness and suppleness of muscle and bone, but Peter felt that if he could keep him in sight, he'd eventually have him. The boy's speed was probably short-run. No doubt he smoked and didn't train. It went with the type.

Peter hadn't run since his beating but that was no great layoff. His insulated boots and the stiffness in his ankle, though, slowed him somewhat. He set a pace that kept the boy in view but wouldn't build up an oxygen debt.

The boy darted between two parked cars and ran across the street. As he crossed, Peter glimpsed the Jaguar pacing him. Good girl. At the corner of the block, the boy, gaining slightly, ran left at a narrower and darker street. Peter picked up his pace. The boots were really holding him back and the bulky pea coat was no help either.

The boy glanced back and bounced a sharp right angle across the street and into an alley. Peter was fearful of losing him and cursed his stupidity for not anticipating that the boy would be wary and regard Peter as a threat.

Peter stopped at the alley. It was narrow across but ran back deep to the side of a third building. He couldn't tell whether the end was blocked by a fence or whether it was open to the left or right. It was classic alley, dark, ominous, and trash-canned.

Conceding he was probably being twice foolish, he started down it, his senses supertuned, his movements cautious. He had probably lost the boy if it opened to the right or left at the end. His only chance was that he was hiding by trash cans and would try to bolt past him.

Peter glanced back. The Jaguar had pulled up and was idling. He knew that when he got back to it, he was in for a lecture from Nancy on insanity, immaturity, and stupidity.

He saw him about fifteen feet ahead. A foot was splayed out from behind a barrel. The end of the alley must be blocked, which meant the boy would try to get past Peter. He wondered why the boy had come in here; it didn't seem a smart move. Probably fear bordering on panic. No doubt he figured he was next on the list, ticketed to go the way of his buddy.

"Hey, Deleo." Peter called the name softly. He wished he knew the first name. He kept his eye on the foot but it didn't move. He took another step forward.

"Deleo." He checked behind himself again. Nancy was looking in anxiously.

"Hey, kid, I just want to talk."

He took another two steps forward. He wondered if the boy had a knife. He had to be prepared for that possibility. Then the thought that this might not be Deleo struck him. But it had to be. It had been written all over his face just before he bolted.

"Look, I just want to help."

The foot moved. He was preparing to lunge out.

Peter moved in quickly in a semi-crouch, his arms spread. The boy came out low, trying to slip under Peter's arms. Peter grabbed the jacket, felt the boy slipping out from it, and hugged his arms around the boy's lower chest.

"Easy, easy, I just want to talk."

"Let go, you son of a bitch." The boy turned, twisted, and slammed his fist into Peter's chin. Dropping his head, Peter grabbed the boy's arm, pushed his shoulder into his torso, and forced him to the alley wall. They rattled together with a trash can and fell to the ground. Peter tried to straddle the squirming, wheezing boy.

"Get the hell offa me, you bastard." He arched his legs and bounced Peter back and away. Peter flung himself full length back on top, trying to pin the boy's arms with his knees. He figured maybe he had a fifteen-pound advantage and should be able to hold him down.

"Listen to me, will you?" Peter found it difficult to talk. Again a fist rammed into his face and the wiry body was bucking him up and down and off with the strength of desperation.

Peter didn't want to do it, but the boy was on the verge of breaking away. He slapped the side of the boy's face hard, and when he struck back, slapped again harder.

"Stop it! I don't want to do this. I just want to talk, goddammit." He poised his hand and suddenly the boy went limp, great sobs gushing from his chest.

For several moments they were like that: the boy crying and Peter sitting atop him. Then Peter began to pat the boy's shoulder.

"Take it easy, take it easy. It's okay. No one's going to hurt you." He got up slowly and held out his hand to the boy. "Come on, get up."

Sniffling and averting his eyes from Peter's gaze, the boy did not get up.

"Come on, get up. That ground is cold," Peter said, reaching down and pulling the boy to his feet. The boy slobbered, slow spasms, his head hung down.

"Listen to me," Peter said. He put his hand under the boy's chin and tried to direct his gaze but the boy pulled his head away. He began to bite at his thumbnail.

"Hey, pay attention to me a minute, will you? If I were out to get you, would I be talking this way? I could blast you right here."

The boy stopped worrying his thumb and slowly looked up at Peter.

"I want you to look out to the street. See that car? That's mine. That's a woman in it. I want us to go out to the car where we can talk. That's all. Just talk."

The boy's eyes rolled and he looked as though he was going to bolt.

Peter held his arm. "Look, if I were going to hurt you, would I have a woman as a partner? The latest thing in women's lib to get on a hit squad?" As he said it, he knew the timing was poor for attempts at humor.

"What do you want?" The voice was fearful but not too unsteady now.

"Just to talk."

"What about?"

"Come on." Peter put his arm around the boy's shoulder and led him to the car, watchful lest he try to break away, but he seemed resigned or reassured. Peter couldn't tell which. They got in the back seat.

"Drive."

"Where to?" Nancy's eyes searched them.

"It doesn't matter. Just around."

"You okay?" she asked.

"Fine. We're both fine." Peter looked at the boy. "What's your first name?"

After a moment, the boy mumbled something.

"I didn't get what you said."

"Frankie."

"Frankie, this is Nancy. Nancy, this is Frankie Deleo."

They rode in silence for two or three minutes. Frankie reached into his jacket and pulled out a crumpled pack of Marlboros. Time for the Marlboro Man to reward himself for surviving one of life's traumas, Peter thought wryly. Goddam advertising. Talk about drug pushers.

Frankie lit up, inhaled deeply a couple of times, and said, "Okay, so let's talk." Peter guessed he was reassured by Nancy.

"You pack a pretty good punch there, kid," Peter said, rubbing his jaw.

Frankie looked at him. "Mister, cut the bullshit, huh? What is it you want to talk about?"

"Frankie, you had a friend, Tommy Stella?" Peter kept his voice even.

"I figured it was about that. You're a cop, right?"

"I might as well be one. Everyone seems to think I am. But, no, I'm not."

Frankie digested that for a moment. "How do you know about Tommy?"

"That's not important. I just do."

"Yeah, it is. It's important."

They rode in silence for a few more moments. Frankie sucked deeply on his cigarette a few times and flicked ashes on the floor. Finally, he said, "What do you want to know?"

Peter knew he had to be careful with his wording if he was to get anything. "Frankie, you saw Tommy get picked up the last night he was seen. Is that right?" There was no escaping the bluntness of the words.

Frankie let out his breath slowly. "Geez, I knew I shouldna told my brother. He can't keep his trap shut."

"Okay, okay, don't worry about it. The world doesn't know. And you don't have to worry about me, about us. We tell no one about you or anything you say." Peter felt a twinge of guilt. Did the boy know that many already knew about him?

"Why do you want to know, then, if you got no one to report this to?"

They were stopped at a red light and Peter could tell the boy was becoming anxious again. He was ready to reach out and grab him if he tried to jump out. He waited for the green light and the Jag to get rolling before he spoke.

"Frankie, I understand you saw your buddy being taken to Oak Way Cemetery."

"Uh-uh. No."

"No?"

"No. I seen these two gorillas grab Tommy, so I follows them as far as Oak Way Avenue. That's all."

"You didn't see them take Tommy to the cemetery?"

"No way. I got as far as Oak Way Avenue and I turned around."

"Oak Way Avenue doesn't lead to much besides the cemetery, does it?"

Frankie shrugged.

"Why did you turn around?"

"Jesus, what the hell am I talking to you for?" Frankie's
voice quavered and Peter knew he was crying again.

Peter put his arm on his shoulder. "Frankie, I'm sorry, I really am. There was nothing you could do to help Tommy." He
could feel the boy's body shaking.

"I left him. I shouldna left him. What a brave bastard I am.
I got scared, so I turned around." He looked at Peter with reddened eyes. "They're gonna get me, I know they are, 'cause I
opened my big mouth." Frankie ran his fingers through long,
dark hair.

"Easy, easy, take it easy," Peter said softly.

"Mister, who the hell are you, anyway? And her? What's
this to you?"

Peter sat back and rubbed his hands together contem-
platively. This was probably going to be foolish. "Okay,
Frankie, I'll level. I think something screwy's going on at that
cemetery. A friend of mine—no way connected with Tommy—
was last known to be at Oak Way Cemetery doing some jogging. She's not been heard from since. That's why it's important to me to know if Tommy was actually taken there."

Frankie regarded Peter thoughtfully a moment, then looked
out the window as they rode. They were on a long, lonely
street, barren as a plain on both sides except for an occasional
large warehouse set well back.

Frankie spoke very softly. "Me and Tommy worked after
school for Mr. Scalise at his food store. One night, about three
weeks ago, I guess, these two gorillas came in after him and
took him away. They didn't see us but I swear it was the same
two that grabbed Tommy. Anyways, Tommy followed them.
He told me later that they took Mr. Scalise to Oak Way Cemetery." Frankie stopped talking for a few moments and Peter
was about to say something when Frankie began again. "They
killed Mr. Scalise, Tommy said. Tommy saw it. He didn't give

me no details or nothing, but it was really bothering him. The night those two goons got Tommy we was supposed to meet and he was gonna tell me all about it. But I was a couple of minutes late and . . ." His voice trailed off. Frankie took out a handkerchief and blew his nose loudly into it, then dabbed at his eyes.

"Tommy figured these guys spotted him and I know he was scared." Frankie looked at Peter. "Jesus, what a goddam hero I am, huh? I mean, first I'm late and Tommy gets nabbed and then I don't even help him."

Frankie laid his head back on the seat. Tears rolled down to his upper lip, and he caught them with his tongue. He swallowed deeply several times.

Peter looked at Nancy. She appeared to be concentrating on driving but in the rearview mirror he could see that her eyes were moist.

So there it was. Now he knew that Ricky got it at Oak Way. Tommy almost certainly did, and Alison was last known to be there. Now what?

"Frankie, you know what you have to do, don't you?" The boy's head was still resting on the seat as he stared through bubbling eyes at the Jag's headlining. "You've got to go to the police and see if you can identify those guys from mug shots."

Frankie slowly turned his head to look at Peter. "No way." His voice sounded as if he were out of breath. "You said you wouldn't tell anyone."

"I won't. But I think you should. It seems pretty obvious that something's going on at that cemetery."

Frankie looked out the window, opened it, took a last drag, and threw out his cigarette. For a moment he didn't shut the window and cold air buffeted in.

"Take me home, huh?"

Peter nodded to Nancy's eyes in the mirror. She pulled to the side and made a U-turn.

"What about Tommy? For him, don't you want to do something about those guys?" Peter didn't want to say that, to deepen Frankie's feelings of guilt, but it was necessary.

Frankie did not reply and for several minutes they rode with no sound but the slip of air against the window moldings and Frankie's short, quick sniffles. They were out of the plains and back in the narrow streets when he blew his nose again and said, "Mister, you gotta promise that you won't mention my name to the cops. 'Cause if you do, I'll deny that I ever even talked to you. You want me to say it, I'll say it: I'm scared shitless of those guys. My brother says I stay low and keep my mouth shut, everything's probably okay. That's what I'm going to do."

He leaned over and said to Nancy, "Take your next right and let me off at the corner, okay?"

As Nancy stopped at the corner, Peter said, "Frankie, I think you're wrong, but I understand how you feel and I promise you I won't mention you to the cops." He touched the boy's sleeve. "I might want to get in touch with you again, okay? My name is Peter and I'm a friend."

Frankie muttered something and shook his head. "Yeah," he said as he got out of the car.

They watched him walk away. The swagger was gone and he seemed small and vulnerable. Peter got into the front seat behind the wheel. They went back to Boston by the Sumner Tunnel and were almost through it before Nancy spoke.

"Well, I guess the probabilities you asked about a while ago are different from what I thought."

"I guess."

"That poor kid. He seemed so tough when he came up to you on the street. But then . . ."

"I know. He's scared and he's on a guilt trip. I'm worried about him. I hope they don't get to him. Actually, he's probably right. If he keeps his mouth shut, they'll let him alone. At least that's what Joey seemed to think. Still . . ." He shook his head.

"What were you going to say?"

"I don't know. I hate to sound corny, raise the old civic responsibility bit, but . . ."

"Oh, God, Peter, what can you do?"

"First thing in the morning I'm going back to see that cop I talked with. But I won't mention Frankie's name."

"Do you think the police can do anything?"

"No. There's still not much concrete to go on. But what else can I do? I don't know."

"I owe you an apology."

"For what?"

"For thinking you were making connections where there were none."

"Aw, shucks."

"Actually, I'm very proud of you. You were very nice with that boy. Tender, even."

"Double shucks."

They were out of the tunnel. The Boston skyline loomed, somehow warm and comforting.

"Let's go over to Cityside for a Reuben and some chili," Nancy suggested.

"Sure," Peter said, even though he didn't feel much like eating. He was wound up and his jaw ached. He wasn't lying when he had said Frankie packed a good punch.

Lieutenant Gabriel listened patiently as Peter told him of the additional connections to the cemetery and, when Peter finished, he lit a Pall Mall from the open pack on his desk. He regarded Peter carefully a moment.

"Mr. Swann, I don't know what you've been up to. Playing Sherlock Holmes, I guess. And I don't know where you got your information. You say you can't reveal the source."

"It wouldn't do any good. The source would deny ever telling me anything."

"Yeah, okay, we'll come back to that, but first things first. You're a nice-looking young guy. You seem sensible. But you are fooling around with some very dangerous people, Mr. Swann. They get wind of your meddling around and you too will be in never-never land."

Lieutenant Gabriel picked up a pad of yellow lined paper from his desk and with a tooth-marked cheap plastic ballpoint, ink down to the last quarter inch, scratched something onto the paper.

"Okay, so here's what you have or think you have." He looked at the pad. "One. Bradley girl goes jogging at Oak Way Cemetery and disappears. Two. Americo Scalise, you say, was witnessed getting the death kiss at Oak Way." He looked up at Peter. "By the way, we did know that Mr. Scalise was among the missing, presumed dead. Trouble is, as far as we are concerned, no bod. No complaint from anyone, not from his wife, not from his children. But those things have a way of getting found out. At least unofficially. Anyway"—he looked at his pad and took a draw on his Pall Mall—"number three. This we didn't know. And if it's as you say, it's really strange. I can understand the silence about Ricky. He was involved, a consenting adult. But a kid? That's unusual, code or no code. Still, the parents might not come forward. At least not to us. Fear's a powerful thing, Mr. Swann, and these people know enough to be fearful. That tell you something about your own messing around?"

Peter shrugged noncommittally.

"I don't know if you're brave or foolish, Mr. Swann." He looked at his pad again. "Anyway, I'll check with Chelsea P.D. to see if there's been anything on this Stella kid."

Lieutenant Gabriel leaned forward. "Now let's get back to this witness you are trying to protect. He's probably in trouble and the best thing you could do is tell us who he is so that we could protect him."

"How are you going to do that? And for how long? I think that's the point. He knows that if the police are seen around him that's a sign that he's talked to you and once you're gone . . ."

"This source of yours actually didn't witness anything directly, you say."

"That's correct."

"It's not hard to figure that it was one of Tommy's friends. Which one wouldn't be too hard to find either, but as you say, he probably would tell us nothing."

Lieutenant Gabriel took a deep drag on his cigarette and smiled humorlessly at Peter. "So, Mr. Swann, what do you—what do we—have? A big fat nothing. Hearsay evidence by way of you from a party that won't say anything to us anyway."

Peter started to speak but Lieutenant Gabriel interrupted. "You are assuming, no doubt, that something sinister is going on at Oak Way, that it's a hiding place for underworld contracts, that they're burying them there. That's really not all that new. Joe Bananas used to do something like that, I think. But we have nothing concrete to go on. We can't just go marching out there with a bulldozer and start digging up all the graves. Do you know how many graves are there, Mr. Swann? That was an operating cemetery from well before the American Revolution. And what's the connection with the Bradley girl, which is what got you started in the first place?"

"Maybe she witnessed a killing or something."

Lieutenant Gabriel exchanged the Pall Mall for the ballpoint and bit into it. He studied Peter's face without the cynicism that Peter had felt the first time he had talked with him about Alison.

"Mr. Swann, let me say this right off. Your coming in here like this, concerned and all, is a refreshing change from the usual apathy we deal with. The general public usually doesn't give a shit about stuff like this unless it's affecting them directly. Which is where they make a mistake, actually. It affects them anyway, but I don't want to get up on that no-man-is-an-island soapbox right now.

"Despite all this stuff you hear about crime prevention," Gabriel continued, "police usually can do nothing but react, Mr. Swann, after the fact. See, our hands are tied by laws protecting certain rights, which is all well and good, but, well, you know what I mean. We have to have concrete reason to move in on something and so far in this matter that you have raised, we don't have that."

A young plainclothes cop stuck his head into the doorway of Lieutenant Gabriel's cubicle. Gabriel looked up. "Yeah,

Bobby, the usual. Get Mr. Swann here a coffee too. How do you like it? Regular? Get him a regular coffee. Doughnut too."

Peter said nothing. He hadn't run yet and didn't particularly want the coffee and doughnut.

"What do you do for a living, Mr. Swann, if you don't mind me asking?"

"Until recently, I taught high school English."

"Oh, that sounds interesting."

"Really? I've noticed when I used to tell people I teach English—at a cocktail party, let's say—why, they'd be all over me vying for my attention. Regular celebrity."

Lieutenant Gabriel smiled. "I didn't mean to sound condescending."

"You didn't. I was just indulging in some poor irony. Actually, teaching has its moments but it can be rather dull."

"You said, 'taught.' "

"Yeah. I got lucky. I won the lottery."

Lieutenant Gabriel arched his eyebrows. "Ve-ry nice. So that means now you've got all kinds of time to keep interested in this Oak Way thing."

"Lieutenant Gabriel, please, I've been all through that. I suppose you can take back all those nice things about my being civically responsible. Now we can write it off as foolhardiness born from boredom." He saw no point in divulging his feelings for Alison.

"Not at all. But I'll be perfectly honest. You should just forget this whole thing. Like right now. If you keep sniffing around, like I said before, you don't know what they might try to do to you."

Peter stood up. "Well, Lieutenant Gabriel, if I disappear, then you'll know I was on to something, won't you?"

"I didn't say you weren't. I simply said that at this point there is nothing for the police to make any kinds of moves about." He watched Peter move to the doorway. "Where are you going, Mr. Swann? Aren't you going to have your coffee and doughnut?"

"No, thank you, Lieutenant. I'm going running now and I

don't need that particular ballast. Some other time, perhaps."

"Sure. And, Mr. Swann?"

"Yes?"

"Watch yourself. I *am* interested but at this point that's all I can be." He handed Peter a card. "Here's a number that can get through to me most any time. Give me a call if you stumble across something, if you hear something new. But, Mr. Swann, don't go looking for it."

After Peter left, Lieutenant Gabriel waited for his coffee and doughnut and stared at the yellow paper he had written on.

Then he made a phone call to Chelsea.

CHAPTER 11

The phone was ringing when Peter got back to his apartment.

"Hello, Peter? Joey." The call was unusual, unique, in fact. Peter couldn't recall Joey Blowtorch ever calling him on the phone.

"What's up, Joey?"

"I ought to ask you the same thing."

"I've been busy."

"Yeah, that's why I'm calling, Peter. You know me for a up-front guy, right?"

Peter mumbled an assent to the rhetorical question. Clark jumped onto the table with the phone and wound himself back and forth against Peter's arm.

"I say what I think, so I ain't gonna beat around the bush. I probably shouldn't be talking to you, but we go back a ways, don't we, Peter?"

Peter went along. "Yeah, we do, Joey," he said as he rumpled Clark's ears.

Joey's voice lowered and became confidential. "Peter, what the hell you been up to? You know better, for crying out loud. Things you hear at Sam's, well, you just got to take them with a grain of salt. Let'm go in one ear and out the other."

"Joey, I know why you called."

"Yeah?"

"Yeah. You've been taking a course in clichés and want me to get in on it."

"Huh?"

"Nothing. You said you weren't going to beat around the bush. You're wearing a groove around it."

"Peter, some friendly advice. I hear things. I'm gonna say it once but I shouldn't have to say it at all. You should know better. You know how things work with . . . But, mind you, I've never talked with you."

Peter knew what was coming and said nothing.

"Peter, just butt outa anything you heard about Ricky Scalise or the kid who worked for him. Matter a fact, if I was you, I would just take off for a while to someplace nice and warm to demonstrate that you understand you've been a bad boy and have learned a lesson."

Peter wondered whether the advice was simply friendly concern or whether Joey had been officially delegated to convey it. Probably it was from just Joey. He had said he would disclaim the call.

"Thanks, Joey. I understand what it means for you to call me. I appreciate it. And I also understand that you never called."

"Okay, Peter. I sure hope I got through to you."

There was a click and the other end went dead.

Peter took his time changing into his running things. Then he washed out Clark's bowl and gave him some dry pellets that he was partial to, shaped like miniature zebras, gazelles, and other prey straight from the Serengeti.

He sat by the kitchen counter and watched and listened to Clark crunch his way through his snack, pausing occasionally between bites to look up and around in the nervous fashion of cats.

The call from Joey had been unsettling, especially following Lieutenant Gabriel's admonition. For the first time, he felt a real fear that he might have ventured into ominous regions, like the closets and cellars of childhood nightmares where legs churn impotently and the voice is paralyzed.

Last night, after scuffling and talking with Frankie, he had been a long time unwinding. He had had the feeling he was closing in on something, that he could contribute to the destruction of a malignancy, and the feeling was heady. Vietnam had never felt like that. That had been just malignant, something you couldn't contain or cope with. You just tried to survive it.

But now a sense of the helplessness and hopelessness that had been Nam pervaded him. He was dealing with an evil that did not define itself conveniently or separate itself clearly from its milieu. As in Nam, the enemy here, osmosis-like, spread into the general community. In a sense, Nancy had been right about that. You couldn't hack away the cancer because it had a symbiotic relationship with its grateful host.

Should he say to hell with it? Frankie wouldn't help himself. Ricky Scalise's wife and kids weren't speaking up. But what about Alison?

"This is a basic dilemma, Clark, old boy," he said, putting the cat out the back door to the neat little yard that was mostly brick-in-sand patio with a splash of grass and some flower beds. A high fence all around secluded the yard pretty much from the closed-in houses. Clark would stay there while he ran, explore the bushes hopeful for a bird, and then come in for the day when Peter returned. He was not a roamer and an hour or so in the great outdoors satisfied whatever atavistic urges temporarily overcame the desire for security, relative warmth, and a soft chair.

Peter locked up and began his run. It was his first since the alley incident, not counting his brief pursuit of Frankie last night, and he planned to run just three or four miles so that he wouldn't push the injured ankle too quickly. He was prone to Achilles tendon problems. But the ankle felt so good, he felt so good, that he did his usual eight and then doubled back and did four more. Nice ring to that: twelve, an even dozen.

This was the good life, he thought. Free to do this. Why was he complicating things? Why not drop the whole matter and enjoy his good fortune, enjoy the liberation his winnings had given him? A million dollars. The state liked to promote that as making him a millionaire. But it wasn't quite that. Fifty thousand a year for twenty years, a big chunk less after taxes.

Not really easy street, but no complaints from one accustomed to an English teacher's salt.

As he returned home, running up Charles Street, Peter felt the exhilaration of a long run nearing its completion, heightened by a resolution to take on no more burdens, to indulge in no more crusades. From now on he would move with the wind of his fancy; he could do far worse than running, reading, and Nancy Brewer.

He checked the two lanes of oncoming traffic and crossed Charles. As he ran by the row of parked cars just before veering left up Mount Vernon, the maroon Pontiac idling by the curb, with a short chirp from its tires, suddenly shot forward.

Peter had no place to go but up onto the scant hood of a parked Horizon. The Pontiac's fender nudged his right calf and slanted off the side of the Horizon. Metal scratched against metal and the juddering Horizon threw Peter to the sidewalk. He bounced up and watched the Pontiac skitter for a moment, and then pick up speed and disappear. He assured the quickly gathering crowd that he was all right and that he had gotten the license number.

He tested his leg and ran up Mount Vernon to his apartment. As he went to the kitchen to write down the license number, he felt the cold draft. The inside window over the sink was wide open and the outside storm window had been cleanly broken so that no jagged edges would cut whoever had crawled in.

A quick inspection of the apartment revealed nothing amiss or damaged. He went to the back door and clucked twice. Giving up a position of concealment under a rhododendron, Clark ran to the door.

"Clark, how would you like a bull mastiff for a living companion?"

He dialed the number Lieutenant Gabriel had given him, waited through four rings before a voice answered.

"Eleven. Officer Cahill."

"May I have Lieutenant Gabriel, please."

"Your name, please, sir?"

"Swann. S-w-a-n-n."

Peter waited a moment before the voice of Lieutenant Gabriel broke the mechanical oblivion of the hold button.

"Yes, Mr. Swann."

Peter wanted to present this well. He hoped he didn't sound like an old lady. "Lieutenant, I don't know whether there is any connection between what we discussed this morning and what just happened, but I thought it might be advisable for you to know."

He told Lieutenant Gabriel of the Pontiac and the forced entry to his apartment.

"You got the license number?"

"Yes. Massachusetts 428 NKX."

"Mass 428 Nora Kilo X-ray. Wait a minute." Another moment of hold, punctuated by the faint hum and scratch of electrical process.

Abruptly, the voice came back. "Yeah, stolen early this morning, Mr. Swann—'79 maroon Bonneville, from South Boston. You get a look at the occupants?"

"Two males. But beyond the general impressions of their being white, age anywhere between twenty-five and forty, and tough-looking, I couldn't tell you any more. Oh, yeah, except that the driver looked as though he was pretty big. Hard to tell on that, because it was a quick glimpse and naturally he was seated."

"You said 'tough-looking'?"

"Yeah, you know. They didn't look like Harvard Square or State Street."

"Could you see how they were dressed?"

Peter wondered about the relevance of that. What difference did it make? Clothes could be changed. "Not really. All I got was a quick look at their faces."

"Hair color? Complexion?"

"Ordinary. They weren't blond or red-headed. Dark brown hair, I guess. Average length. Not much help, huh?"

"No. But the circumstances weren't very good, were they?"

There was a pause and Peter's guess that a Pall Mall was

being lighted was confirmed by the rush of air in the earpiece.

"Okay, Mr. Swann, now you say that apparently nothing was taken from your apartment?"

"Apparently."

There was another pause, another rush of air.

"Of course, it could be coincidence, but my guess, Mr. Swann, is that you have been twice warned. If they really wanted to get you, they could have. This is a way—two ways, actually—to tell you that there are any number of things that could be done to stop you from nosing around. Do you have any pets?"

The question startled Peter. "Yes, a cat."

"He wasn't hurt?"

"He was outside."

"Lucky cat. Otherwise you probably would have found him in your toilet or bathtub or sticking half out of your garbage disposal."

Peter looked down at Clark tentatively poking at the swaying cord.

"I'll have someone by in fifteen minutes to take a statement, Mr. Swann."

"Is that it? I mean, there's nothing—"

"We'll look for the car, of course, but by now it's been abandoned. We'll find nothing in it and your apartment will be clean too. Could anyone have seen your window being broken?"

"Not likely. The back of the place is pretty secluded."

"Mr. Swann, be grateful. I know how that sounds, but, believe me, in a sense you are very lucky."

Peter bit back a retort. He could feel anger and indignation rising, but knew that it was pointless to misdirect them against Lieutenant Gabriel.

After he hung up, he sat for a few moments, petting Clark. Then he took a quick shower and waited for the police.

He gave his report to two young, uniformed officers who several times cautioned him to have his leg checked out even though it felt all right. Finally, to appease them, he assured them that he would, even though he had no intention of doing so.

When they had gone, he made himself coffee, put on a Julian Bream album, and forced himself to concentrate on the lilt of the classical guitar. Usually the effect was almost hypnotically tranquil but now he could not contain the feelings that seemed to rise from his gut and expand to the top of his skull. He had been put upon and the arrogance of the intrusion, calculated to produce fear, was generating rage.

"Goddammit. Those bastards. Who the hell do they think they are?" His voice rose. He knew he sounded foolish but he felt better anyway. Clark, in repose like a paperweight on the rug, paws folded under him, twitched his ears and prepared for retreat.

Peter drained his coffee, shut off the stereo, and carefully returned Julian Bream to his folder. He put on his pea jacket and black knit cap, and carefully locking up as he went out, despite the essential futility of the action, strode with purpose to the Jaguar.

He felt a quick apprehension as he wondered whether they had gotten to it too. It appeared untouched but he looked under it and then opened the hood. Everything seemed in order. No bombs as far as he could tell, but he guessed they could probably make them the size of a ballpoint pen and in the labyrinth of wire, hose, and plumbing under the Jag's hood one could be hidden almost anywhere.

Bracing himself and feeling a bit derring-do, he turned the ignition. The twin-cam six ground its reluctance for about eight seconds before catching and bouncing the tach up to twelve hundred. No explosion. He had been spared oblivion.

As he started to pull out, he saw Andrew leading Mrs. Beauchesne around the corner toward him. On impulse, he got out of the car and went to her. He exchanged the required pleasantries and scratched Andrew's ears before asking whether she had seen anyone by his back window. From the back of her house, she would have a scant view of his yard, what the fence would allow.

"Oh, my goodness, Peter, no, I didn't. What happened? Don't tell me, I can guess. You were broken into, weren't you?"

He nodded.

Mrs. Beauchesne's hands fluttered to her bosom, yanking Andrew's front paws off the ground a bit. "Oh, dear me. I'm telling you, Peter, that's just the limit. When did it happen?"

He told her.

"No, I'm sorry to say that all that time I was brushing Andy and doing his nails. I have to keep at them because, not being let out, he doesn't wear them down much. *I* keep him secured. Not like some of these dogs that roam loose and all. Anyway, Peter, of course I wouldn't have any reason to look over into your yard, and even if I did, the fence pretty much obscures the view." She looked over at the idling Jaguar. "You're going to the police, now, I suppose."

"No. They've already been by. Actually, I'm just on my way out to Oak Way Cemetery."

Mrs. Beauchesne gave a little start. "Oh, Peter, really? Would you mind terribly if I came with you? Mr. Beauchesne is buried there and I just don't get by as often as I'd like. Now you tell me if it's a bother and I'll understand perfectly. Perhaps you're not coming back directly."

Peter hesitated for just a moment. Actually, he hadn't clearly defined his reason for going to the cemetery. He was looking for whatever it might have to tell him but admitted that his motivation was probably anger. But it was most definitely something else too. He felt guilty for giving up on Alison.

"It's no bother. I'd be glad to take you."

As they rode out, Peter knew that, at the very least, Mrs. Beauchesne's feet must have been chilly but she gave no sign, chatting amicably and showing an animation that exceeded even her usual cheerfulness. Peter guessed that she didn't get out much and that this was something of a lark for her. Apparently for Andrew it was a first, as he bounced about the back seat from window to window emitting little high-pitched whistles and whines at whatever piqued his dog interests and values.

Mrs. Beauchesne amused and amazed him with her knowledge of places and points that they passed. She knew Boston. Had lived there all her life, she told him. She was descended from a Salem sea captain who had come to Boston with an established fortune and a liking for the gentility of Beacon Hill but had had a hard time gaining acceptance. "You know that old saying about the Cabots and the Lodges. That's the way it was, a tough city to break into."

When they got to Oak Way Avenue, Peter watched carefully to see whether there was anything else besides the cemetery that would be a likely destination for those who had brought Tommy Stella out here. Frankie hadn't followed the car as far as the entrance, so Peter didn't know for sure that they went into the cemetery itself.

So far the road appeared innocuous. Tree-lined, solid-middle-class residential but not too heavily built up. After a half mile, one side of the road gave way to the cemetery, bordered by a high, ornate wrought-iron fence. After almost another half mile, they came to the main entrance. Peter had hoped to explore Oak Way Avenue beyond the entrance but that could wait until he was alone. He pulled in and was confronted by a large rotary of grass and dug-up, lumped, frozen dirt which in the spring would be ablaze with flowers. The small brick caretaker's cottage was in front of him and the road branched off in three directions.

"Which way is it to Mr. Beauchesne's grave?"

"Oh, you do your business first, Peter, then I'll show you. By the way, you didn't tell me who you wanted to pay respects to. Family?"

"A friend I was in Vietnam with," he lied. He had no plan beyond a general reconnoiter but now he would have to pick a grave to stand by and hang his head.

He took the road leading to the right. It wound down a hill

to an intersection. He took a right again and drove slowly. Three roads over to the left he saw a cemetery truck and crew busy at something. Should he drive by to check? No, the chances were it was innocent. This was a functioning cemetery, and even if something were out of order, at least 90 percent of what went on here must be legitimate, he told himself.

The road curved and sloped gently at first and then rather steeply. Ahead, at the foot of the hill, the larger of the cemetery's two ponds nestled among overleaning trees and shrubs. It was no wonder people liked to jog here. The place was beautiful and Peter could imagine that when the foliage was in bloom it would be gorgeous.

The road leveled and forked, running both directions around the pond. It was good-sized but there would be no way a car could go into it without leaving obvious signs. He stayed with the right side of the fork, the circumference road. Bushes leaned out, scratching the side of the Jaguar.

"I don't think I've ever been down this far," said Mrs. Beauchesne. "Where's your friend buried?"

"Just around the other side here."

The road was very narrow, one car width, and curved back and forth abruptly, conforming to the edge of the pond. With bushes in foliage, the turns would be blind.

A runner popped around a curve and waved as Peter pulled over and stopped. He had a good pace and Peter watched him in the mirror a moment. Andrew stood up in the rear window and growled at the receding figure.

Around the curve and over a small cement bridge the road elevated again sharply. Halfway up the hill between the road and the pond another crew worked at an open grave. They paid the Jaguar no more than cursory attention.

Doug had said that during the day many people ran in the cemetery. Alison had run after dark. If she had stumbled onto something, that suggested that whatever dirty business was being conducted was done after dark. That made sense. Dirty business was usually done after dark. Unless, of course, it was done in such an open way that suggested it was something natural and normal, something that was *supposed* to be done. Like digging graves. If that was the case, why would Alison be regarded as a threat but not the many other runners? Because no one does work at night in a cemetery, he supposed. Therefore, such activity would call attention to itself and she would have investigated.

Most certainly, he knew, he was going to see nothing he shouldn't see out here. Not during the day. But at night? After dark? That's when Alison was here, after dark. If a reconnoiter was to be meaningful, it would have to be after dark. But he had noticed a sign at the main entrance that said the gates were closed after dark. That meant it would have to be on foot. Well, why not? Alison had been on foot.

He felt the chill of fear again, then guilt as he thought of Alison. He would think about coming out here but knew that that concession was tantamount to acknowledging that he *would* come out. He knew he had to.

At the top of the hill, he remembered his ostensible mission and looked for a grave with a flag. He saw one set well back and stopped. "I'll be just a minute," he said as he got out. He walked across the crusty ground to the grave, a flat bronze plaque marker with a flag fluttering slowly on a short iron pole. He read the marker. The man had served in World War II and Korea and had died three years ago at fifty-five. Peter wondered for a moment about the man and how he had felt about war. World War II was supposed to have been different from Nam. Men had wanted to serve. But not so with Korea. It was Korea that caused Ike to come up with the Universal Code. He stood another minute, wondering whether someday he would have a plaque, before going back to the car.

Mrs. Beauchesne was respectfully quiet but Andrew put his paws up on the back of Peter's seat, wiggling and wagging a greeting. He was enjoying this excursion and Peter knew he had made a friend.

"Now, let's see, Peter. I'm a little confused. I've never gone to Mr. Beauchesne's grave from this direction. We always take a left at the caretaker's cabin."

"This outer road just makes a loop. I'll continue along and maybe you'll recognize something."

The road ran rather straight now for almost a half mile before bending left back to the main entrance. They drove past a tall marker and statue of a Union soldier keeping vigil over a large plot set off by a low cement wall.

"It should be right along here, Peter. I recognize that Civil War section. Yes, go left here. Althea Path. Mr. Beauchesne is just down here a ways."

The small road to the left ran in front of the Union soldier, his fifteen-foot bulk keeping eternal duty. Over the low wall, Peter could see that all of the markers were embedded flat and nearly obscured by the ground. Past the wall, standing alone, a tall, weathered, ornate marker caught his eye and he stopped.

"Look at that one," he said. It read:

Lawrence Grayson

Died Andersonville Prison

Nov. 24 1864 20 yrs. 2 mos. 11 days

"Yes. I've noticed that one many times, Peter. It would be easy to become maudlin here, wouldn't it?"

"Yes." He pulled ahead and drove about one hundred yards, until Mrs. Beauchesne signaled him to stop.

"It's right over there, Peter."

He helped her out of the car and across the uneven, frozen ground but hung back respectfully while she stood over her husband's grave. He could see her name and date of birth were also inscribed on the marker by her husband's, a type of foresight and preparedness that he thought bordered on the grisly. She was seventy-six and did very well for her years. She stood for a few moments before turning to him. She was smiling.

"Thank you, Peter, for taking me out here. It makes me feel sad but good at the same time. Do you know what I mean?"

"Yes, I do." He helped her back to the car, glad that he had brought her out here.

"It's strange," she said, settling back in her seat, "but the Carmichael plot just beyond ours looks as if a spot had been dug up not too long ago."

Peter mumbled a preoccupied response as he started the car. He was anxious to finish the loop around the cemetery and explore Oak Way Avenue where it ran beyond the main entrance. He would take Mrs. Beauchesne home and return for that.

"But I know the family and there's no one left. Kate Carmichael was buried, let me see, it must be going on ten years ago."

Peter turned off the ignition. "What did you say?"

"I said that the Carmichael plot looks to be disturbed but as far as I know they're all long dead and buried."

"Excuse me," Peter said, getting from the car. His pulse quickened as he walked past the marker for Mr. and Mrs. Beauchesne and found the Carmichael stone. The turf had indeed been disturbed and laid back again. It was difficult to tell precisely how long ago, but the seams in the grass hadn't filled back in nor had the ground fully settled to hide the outline of a grave. Obviously, it had been done sometime since the fall.

He checked the marker. There were six Carmichaels.

The most recent burial was Katherine Carmichael, 1973.

CHAPTER 12

"You don't learn, do you?"

"Nancy, really, I expected more support from you." Peter washed a pepper, split it open, cleaned it out, and put half of it on the cutting board beside the diced onions and mushrooms.

"Support for what? Getting yourself killed? And maybe me in the process if I'm with you."

"Like now, I suppose?"

"Well, why not? I mean, you read about such things."

"What do you think my would-be assassins are going to do, hover outside your window in a helicopter?"

"How about if they just marched right in the building?"

"With violin cases, I suppose. You do have security here."

"Oh, geez. We've got one old guy down there who must be pushing seventy. But this is a pointless discussion. You know what I mean. You said yourself that Lieutenant Gabriel said you were being warned."

They worked in silence a few moments, Peter at the pepper, Nancy at the tomato sauce for their pizza. Each sensed that the conversation was an incipient quarrel.

"The dough is ready to spread," she said.

"Okay." He rinsed his hands under the faucet and with an old, long plastic drinking tumbler rolled out the dough onto a rectangular pan. Nancy spread the sauce, which she had made from scratch, as she had with the dough also. Onto that she sprinkled a thick layer of grated mozzarella and cheddar and the onions, mushrooms, and pepper that Peter had diced. She put the pizza into the oven and set the timer.

"Want another beer?" she asked.

"I've already got them out."

"Did you get me a Lite?"

"You want a Lite?"

"Yeah. If it's good enough for Bubba Smith, it's good enough for little ol' me."

They sat at her small kitchenette table and sipped awkwardly, neither wanting to broach the topic again. Finally Nancy said, "So how do you think the Celtics will do?"

They both laughed. Nancy hated sports but endured the occasional games that Peter dragged her to.

"Okay," she said, "so hit me with your plan again and forgive me if I remain just a bit incredulous at this whole situation. I mean, really, Peter, it's as if you're saying, 'You get tough with Peter Swann and I'll take on the whole underworld. I'll teach you to try to run me over and break into my apartment and terrorize my poor, innocent cat.'"

"Clark was out and thus spared any trauma." He sipped. "No actual plan. I just figure that if something's going on in that cemetery, it's happening at night. I'm convinced that Alison stumbled onto something that she shouldn't have seen."

"So you will go to the cemetery at night? 'I will go to Korea.'"

"Huh?"

"Don't you remember your history? What Eisenhower said. 'I will go to Korea.' As if he would put his hand on the head of some demon and thereby vanquish it. That's how you're acting. Let's call the press and issue a bulletin: Attention, evil forces at work in the Oak Way Cemetery. You are hereby being given notice. Peter Swann is coming out. Your days, or should I say nights, are numbered."

"Ike stopped the war."

"Poor analogy. I shouldn't have brought it up." She sipped her Lite. "You're going to bring a wooden stake, garlic, and a crucifix, aren't you?"

"Very funny."

"Not so funny. You wouldn't catch me in that place at night even under ordinary circumstances. At least bring a gun."

"I don't have one, you know that."

"Buy one."

"Ha. Do you know what that involves in this liberated Commonwealth? Besides, I don't know where to buy silver bullets."

"What you should do, of course, is go back to Lieutenant Gabriel and tell him about that grave that had been dug up. That's what really got you going, isn't it?"

"Not just that. It would do no good to go back to him. I'm sure that they could come up with a legit-sounding explanation at the cemetery for that grave."

"Like what?"

"I don't know."

"What do you think it really means?"

"I don't know that either."

"Maybe it *is* legit."

"I doubt it."

She drained her beer and went to the refrigerator. "Ready for another?"

"Please."

She sat back down with a Labatt's and a Lite. "When do you plan to engage in this further adventure of Peter Swann?"

"Tomorrow night."

"I'll say this for you. You don't waste time. Have you thought this out? I mean, what you are going to actually do there?"

"I'll wing it. Like Alison. I'll be a night jogger, all innocent as hell, and see what I see."

Nancy swung her crossed leg quickly and twirled a small curl over her ear. "Maybe I've been drinking these beers too quickly, but I will now say that I intend to go with you."

"Like hell."

"Look, we've been through this before, as I recall. Spare me the strong male, weak female role playing, if you please."

"You forget, my pet, that you don't run. Remember? Puritanical self-punishment, you call it. Twentieth-century self-flagellation, I believe, was your clever expression."

"We could walk."

"What the hell kind of cover is that? Two weirdos out for a winter's evening stroll amongst the stiffs."

"Alison was running and that didn't serve as a cover for her, if your theory is correct."

"If my theory is correct, Alison wasn't forewarned of trouble. I am."

"Well, then, I can ride behind you in the car."

"That would look cute. Sonny's afraid of the dark and needs Mommy with a flashlight. Besides, the car's headlights would be a tip-off and stop anything that I might see. Anyway, you can't get the car in after dark. The gates are closed."

"All right. I'll wait outside. If you don't show up after a designated time, I'll go for the cavalry."

"How's the pizza coming?"

"Don't be evasive. The timer's set. Admit it, there's nothing wrong with that idea. It wouldn't blow any so-called cover. Actually, it makes a lot of sense."

Peter grunted into his beer.

"Say yes."

"I guess."

"Oh, this is so exciting. Just like Mr. and Mrs. North."

"We're not married."

"Times have changed. We're still wholesome."

"But you will stay in the car."

"Of course. Just one thing, though."

"What's that?"

"We bring my car. If I'm going to do any sitting around in a car, I want to stay warm."

"There goes the image," Peter said. Nancy had a Monza which she thought was sporty. Peter was unable to sway her to his opinion that it was ordinary.

The timer buzzed.

"Well, let's have our pizza and then make love with wild abandon," she said. "Tomorrow night might be the beginning of the long sleep."

CHAPTER 13

The cat's body thunked down beside Peter's head and startled him into the bewilderment of an abrupt awakening. He sat upright. Bright sunlight was slanting past the drawn shade. The clock read 8:25. He had slept much later than normal.

"Dammit, Clark, some morning one of those leaps will give me cardiac arrest." He leaned back into the pillow and fondled Clark's ears. The cat resonated as he kneaded the blanket with big paws. With his eye, Peter measured the jump from the chest of drawers to the bed. It was considerable.

Peter allowed the luxury of a few minutes' dozing before he forced himself up. He had a busy morning ahead and could not tarry for too long. First, he fed a small can of tuna and egg to Clark and then showered and fed himself.

He intended to build a security base for tonight, although he admitted that what he had in mind was flimsy at best. If indeed he was being kept tabs on, his excursions to Oak Way, yesterday with Mrs. Beauchesne and tonight, could cause apprehension in the wrong circles. But if he could let it be thought that he had learned a lesson, that he had actually been intimidated, then he could increase his odds of non-interference, indeed survival. He knew his jaunts to the cemetery would be stretching coincidence, as Nancy had pointed out, but unless Frankie had talked, which was unlikely, there was no reason for anyone to think his suspicions or questionings had led him to Oak Way. He hoped.

He had misgivings about Nancy coming with him tonight but was grateful for her spunkiness and concern. It was possible he'd need a quick getaway and having her waiting with a running engine could prove prudent, to say the least. But he doubted it would come to anything as dramatic as that. He had no intentions of playing hero tonight. This was simply a scouting foray in the guise of an innocent quest for cardiovascular fitness. Should he see anything suspicious, he would report it to the doubting Lieutenant Gabriel.

Traffic was light as he drove to Sam's for his coffee. Even though he was late, Joey stayed there until midmorning before going home to bed. He felt a certain guilt about using Joey for his planned deception; it was taking advantage of an old friendship. But he had to get the odds in his favor as much as possible.

Peter had thought of, but quickly rejected, Nancy's suggestion of a gun for tonight. He hadn't handled a firearm since Vietnam and on general principle didn't want to again. Besides, what he had used there hadn't been a handgun. In any event, the difficulties of getting a legal handgun in Massachusetts were considerable. He supposed that yesterday's attempt at a hit and run *might* be cause for allowing him a license, but it might not. Frankly, he didn't want to bother to find out.

He had also thought of a knife, a lead pipe, or even a roll of dimes in his fist, but any of these things would be an admission that he was loaded for bear, looking for trouble. So, ultimately, he would rely on prudence and fast feet.

Because it was late, he was able to pull up in front of Sam's without double-parking. Inside, most of the usual throng had long since braced themselves against the rigors of another workday and had gone their ways. There were no filled cups on the counter.

Joey was seated alone at his usual spot drinking coffee and reading the morning *Globe*. Peter thought that he and Sam exchanged glances as he came in.

Peter felt Sam was avoiding his gaze as he poured coffee and he made small talk the way you do with someone you've argued with. Or with someone who is fatally ill.

He brought his coffee to Joey's table and sat down, but Joey did not look up from the *Globe*. He blew on his coffee a moment before sipping. "Cold out," he said.

"Yeah."

Peter sipped.

"Where's Barbie?" He knew but he felt the need to say something innocuous to ease the strain between them.

"She's been in and gone." Joey turned the page in the *Globe*, picked it up a bit from the table, and engrossed himself in an article. Idly, Peter tried to make out the headline but it was convoluted in the folds of the paper.

"I just read an article in here about Ken Baer, center field with the Sox. *Used* to be with the Sox, I should say. Did you know they traded him, Peter?"

"I haven't read the paper yet, Joey."

"He's gone. To Cleveland for a lefty pitcher, kid name a Wright. Trade don't seem to make much sense but the point is, I guess, that Baer wasn't a team player, kinda a troublemaker. Saying stuff that wasn't his business, like criticizing management. He didn't get the big picture, know what I mean? So, even though they didn't like to, the Sox had to get rid of him. Didn't want to, the article said, but *had* to."

Peter understood the parable. "Joey, thanks for the call yesterday. I had a little trouble after you called, don't know whether you heard about it."

For a moment it appeared that Joey wasn't listening, then he said, "Yeah, I heard something about it." His voice was low, his eyes remained on the paper. "Word gets out."

Peter adjusted his seat away from the rays of the sun slanting through the window, a luminous slice of slow-motion smoke and dust motes.

"Peter, what the hell are you doing here?" Even though the words were softly spoken, they slapped at Peter. "Do you listen when people give you a little friendly advice?"

Peter sipped from his Styrofoam cup and leaned into the stream of sun. "That's what I'm trying to tell you, Joey. I'm going to be a good boy and mind my own business." He kept his voice low, his tone confidential. He hoped he was achieving the proper measure of contrition without sounding petulant or false.

Joey looked up from the newspaper and swiveled his eyes around in a furtive sweep. "What the hell are you telling *me* for? Who do you think *I* am, the friggin' godfather or something? Me, I'm a nothing. I keep my ears to the ground and mind my own goddarn business, is all." Joey bent to his newspaper again before continuing. "I already told you what you should do. Get lost for a while."

The words were said with a finality and Peter thought Joey was finished talking. He leaned back, wondering whether his coming here had been ill considered. He knew now that as far as Joey was concerned he was strictly hands-off. Certainly, Joey was not about to scramble like some kind of town crier spreading the word that Peter had seen the light.

Folding his *Globe*, Joey stuck it in the pocket of his jacket, an old rumpled Mighty Mac. "I must be nuts letting myself be seen with you, let alone talking to you." He stood up and then leaned down, his hands on the table, his face close to Peter's. Peter could smell the blend of whiskey and coffee on his breath.

"Somebody gets the idea you didn't get the message, Peter, they get nervous even a little bit about it, then they have only one way of making sure. I mean, I like you, Peter, I know you for an okay guy, but to them you don't count for shit. You're like a piece of crusty old dog crap on the lawn. Just a nuisance to be swept away."

Peter nearly smiled despite Joey's seriousness. "That's almost poetic, Joey, although not very complimentary."

Joey regarded Peter a moment as though he was dealing with an obtuse child. He stood, shrugged his shoulders in dismissal, and strode out.

Peter sat awhile and finished his coffee. So much for the security base. When he got up to leave, Sam, busy behind the counter, avoided his gaze.

Carmine Bubblegum eyed the Jaguar contemptuously. For his dough, it was the kind of thing that smart-ass fags would ride around in, looking down their noses at American iron, thinking they had a corner on brains. The guy who owned this one was for sure a dumb bastard, though. If Carmine had his choice, he'd send this dude on his way but have a little fun with him first.

But the word for now was to just keep an eye on him, to see if he got the point from yesterday's couple of little warnings. He could have got him yesterday real easy. Just a little flick of the steering wheel and he'd have made a sandwich out of those runner's legs. He laughed to himself at that image. Runner's-leg sandwich. Legs served up between two fenders. That was a good one.

After he and Louie had scared Peter yesterday, he thought that would be it. But this morning, he was told to tail Peter today. Why the hell they just didn't dump him now was beyond Carmine. Waste of gas keeping a tab on him. Probably they weren't really worried because he was such a stumble-bum. What was the word on him? Used to be an English teacher? Carmine tittered a little high-pitched mirthless sound as he thought of that.

"Wha' so funny?" Louie Ciuccio said, scrunched down in the passenger's seat of the Cadillac, sunglasses on to protect his eyes from the sun glints off car and store windows. They were parked down the street from Sam's, keeping a watch on Peter's car.

Carmine took the wad of gum from his mouth and stuck in a fresh piece. "Just thinking about our friend in the Jaguar." He pronounced it in three distinct syllables: Jag-u-ar. "He used to be a freaking English teacher, you know that?"

"Yeah?"

They grinned at each other.

"How the hell can a guy do something like that for a living? I mean, poems, stuff like that?"

"Yeah, I could never get that crap when I was in school," Louie said.

"That's 'cause you're a dumb shit."

"Go to hell." Louie Ciuccio sulked a little in his seat. He lit a Camel and blew the smoke into the windshield. "I suppose you could do all that stuff?"

"Sure. It was easy. I was a regular goddam scholar." Carmine worked the gum with his teeth and lips a moment and then blew a pink, glistening bubble. He sucked it back in and blew two small ones in rapid succession, popping each.

"Take book reports," Carmine said. "I used to like those. You'd have to be a brain amputee to screw up a book report. Christ, you wouldn't even have to read the book."

Louie sucked on the Camel. He was uncomfortable with the topic. He had dropped out of school at sixteen, still in the ninth grade. And he couldn't remember ever reading a book.

"You said he *used* to be an English teacher," Louie said.

"Yeah. He won the goddam lottery, imagine that."

Louie grunted something and sucked on the Camel again. Carmine pressed a button, dropping his window three or four inches. "You smoke too much. Bad for you."

"Go to hell."

"Got a real good vocabulary too."

"Up yours. You sound like that English teacher now."

"Hey, I graduated from high school at least. I don't have to just look at the pictures when I read a magazine."

Louie Ciuccio drew deeply on the Camel and slowly blew a long stream of smoke at Carmine's face. Carmine dropped his window further and fanned the smoke out. He considered saying something but decided not to. He knew just how far he could needle Louie, who was too easily provoked.

Carmine had worked with Louie a long time and sometimes the man frightened even him. He was sadistic. He enjoyed his work, was cut out for what he did. Carmine saw the work as part of the business, a steppingstone, he hoped, to better things. So, for now, he followed orders and did what he was told the best way he could. It didn't repulse him but he didn't get his jollies from it either. He figured that Louie, though, really got his kicks when they made a hit.

Carmine watched Joey Blowtorch come out of Sam's, squint into the sun, and look around nervously before striding away. Carmine elbowed the sulking Louie. "Check that."

Louie grunted but sat up.

A few minutes later, Peter came out to the Jaguar.

Carmine blew a big bubble, and Louie, grinning meanly, muttered, "Hey, English teacher . . ."

Carmine pulled the Caddy out to follow the Jaguar.

CHAPTER 14

Peter felt the chance that he would be tailed to the cemetery was high, so he insisted on driving there himself and having Nancy follow him later in her car.

"It's the only way I'll agree to have you along," he told her as he stood by her window while she changed into an outfit suitable for surveillance work. He was dressed and ready to run. Outside, the dark was brightened by illuminated high-rise buildings and the lights from traffic crawling along the central artery and the waterfront.

"If we both drive out together, what happens when I get out to run and you're by yourself if they come by? What'll you do?"

"Dazzle them with my smile?" She came out of her bedroom in black jeans and black turtleneck.

"For chrissakes, Nancy, what do you think this is, a commando mission? Why don't you blacken your face while you're at it?"

She feigned hurt. "I thought I looked pretty snappy. Kind of like a cat burglar."

"Okay, so let's go through this again. I'll leave here, drive to the cemetery, park near the main entrance, and go in and run to see what I can see."

"How are you going to get in if the gate's locked?"

"There's a little side gate that I think stays open. If not, I'll climb the fence." He led her to the sofa, sat her down, and plopped beside her. "You give me five minutes from the time I leave here, then drive out to the cemetery too. If anyone's following me, they won't connect us and I doubt that they know your car, although maybe they do. But that's a chance."

"I could have borrowed Jane Collins' car."

"Never mind. I don't think it's important. Anyway, I want you to drive by the main entrance and see if everything looks okay. See if anyone's waiting outside. They use a black Caddy sedan, I guess. Very unimaginative, huh? Also, be sure to check whether the main entrance has been opened. If it has, that means that probably they've driven inside to check me out."

"And I go for the cops."

"No. I want you to continue along Oak Way Avenue. By the way, when you drive by, don't slow way down or anything. Just go by as you would normally. You know, if the Cadillac is there, don't gape or gawk. Got that?"

"Yes. You're presenting this very well. I bet you were dynamic in the classroom."

"Okay, so actually, no matter what, you are going to keep driving along Oak Way Avenue. The road continues for a little over a quarter mile before turning left to follow the cemetery. Drive to nearly the end of the road, almost a half mile. About two hundred feet from the end, pull over and park right before the second to the last tree."

"The second to the last tree? How do you have this down so pat?"

"I went back out yesterday afternoon after I brought Mrs. Beauchesne home."

Nancy lit a cigarette from a lighter on the coffee table. "Peter, this gets dumber and dumber."

"What do you mean?"

"Well, if you are being followed, as you seem to think, then they probably followed you yesterday to the cemetery. Twice. And now tonight you go back to run in it. I mean, don't you think that looks just a teensy bit suspicious? Unless they dismiss it as necrophilia."

Peter shrugged. "As I was saying, you wait by the second to the last tree. At that point, the road in the cemetery comes close to the street. If no one is on my tail, I'll run up close.

You can tell me how things look by the main entrance. Then either I'll keep running or jump the fence and join you."

Nancy blew smoke. She looked exasperated. "You insist on doing this?"

"Please. Don't start."

"Okay, okay."

He stood up. "Should we run through it again before I go?"

"No." She got up too. "Wait a minute." Picking up her navy blue warm-up jacket, she fished out a chocolate bar from the pocket and handed it to him. Peter could see a couple more in the pocket.

"What's this for?"

"You know. Food. In case . . ."

He laughed and kissed her. "Nancy, talk about melodrama. I'm not going through the Donner Pass, you know."

When she looked crestfallen, he put it in his pocket and kissed her again. "Thanks."

Peter had deliberately parked away from Harbor Towers near the Aquarium so that he could walk back to his car to see whether he was being followed. He didn't expect to see anything and he didn't. No skulking figures in doorways, no black Cadillac. Of course, having to act as though he had no reason to suspect a tail didn't make spotting one any easier.

As he drove, he frequently checked his mirror, again discreetly, and, again, saw nothing. He reviewed his motivations for going back to the cemetery—the Carmichael grave suggested he was on to something—and wondered whether he was behaving foolishly. Certainly, he was behaving inconsistently, wavering between butting in and butting out. Consistency is the hobgoblin of little minds.

And what was the actual danger? Although Peter conceded a real danger, he had at this point committed himself to a course of action. Mainly, he felt that if it came to it he could outrun any assailants, and at night in the terrain of the cemetery, he would make a difficult target for a handgun.

He was almost on Oak Way Avenue itself before he was

free of general traffic and could tell whether he was being followed by any particular car. The only headlights behind him turned to another road and he drove all the way to the cemetery entrance with nothing following.

As he parked under a streetlamp and locked up, he wondered whether he should wait for Nancy to go by. Was she all right? He dismissed his anxiety as senseless worry; no one watching him would have any reason to bother her.

He went to the little side gate beside the main entrance. It pushed open easily, grating loudly on its hinges. He walked into the darkness of overhanging pine branches and enormous rhododendrons. Pine needles slithered and crunched beneath his shoes. A little path quickly led to the asphalt road and rotary in front of the caretaker's cabin.

The cabin was dark, a green shade drawn tight in the big front window protected by a heavy metal grating.

Away from the streetlamp, it was now quite dark. Peter checked the moon, a thin slice, partly obscured by a scattering of clouds. At best, it would give little light. The roads branching away from the cabin were dim slashes that were quickly lost in the blackness.

If anyone was waiting ahead for him, he'd never see them until he was very close, perhaps too close to dodge away, certainly too close to guarantee that he'd be a poor target for a gun. It would be foolish to run. He turned to go back to the car and wait for Nancy. He'd call the whole thing off and rethink his options, perhaps really consider again the smartest one: forget the whole matter completely.

He stopped at the little path that led back out. Who could be waiting for him with a gun? They couldn't have anticipated his coming out here tonight to run and driven ahead of him. That was farfetched. But they *had* been here to get Alison. That is, if his theory was correct. But that was probably just someone who was already here who stumbled on her unaware. That was a key word—unaware. She had been unaware. He wasn't. And if set upon, he could resist more effectively than she had. Then he thought of the alley. His resistance there had been nil.

Peter stood in indecision a moment in the little dark tunnel of evergreen. When he had taught *The Red Badge of Courage* to his juniors, bravery was naturally discussed and whether young Henry Fleming could be called brave. He had, for the most part, fought unthinkingly, his actions more the result of anger, irritation, or conditioned reflex. Peter had insisted that an individual, to be brave, had to be aware and fearful of the danger he was facing and that young Henry, by that definition, was not really brave.

By his own definition, Peter acknowledged he would be brave if he ran now. He could feel himself sinking into an intellectual funk over this whole matter, and before he became immobilized by it all, he decided to act.

Glancing about, he walked back to the little rotary and went through some brief warm-up stretches mainly for his Achilles tendons. He breathed slowly and deeply, trying to ease the bubble of disquiet in his stomach. When he had finished stretching, he set his chronograph, mainly through habit, and then told himself that he might as well check his time for a lap. It could be interesting. It was over a mile and a half around, he remembered someone telling him, maybe Doug. It should take somewhere around eleven minutes.

He hit his stride, running in the same direction he had driven Mrs. Beauchesne, and could tell right away that he was running well. That was funny about running. You never knew until you started how you'd feel. Sometimes when you were tired or stiff before running, once you began, everything felt good—light and alive. Or it could go just the opposite; you'd run with everything heavy and dead just when you thought it wouldn't be.

Tonight he was fast. He was sure that if he wanted to he could crack a mile in five and a half minutes with ease. The best he had ever done was a 5:11 and he bet that he could beat that. For a moment he became so caught up in thoughts of running that he forgot why he was here. Then he conceded that nervousness was contributing to his speed and that running in the dark definitely created the illusion of a faster pace. He wished he could note where he was at five minutes and at five and a half minutes and later check those distances with the car, with Nancy's car, he reminded himself, thinking of the useless instrumentation in the Jaguar. But it was virtually impossible to read the watch while running in the dark.

He was on the long decline that led to the pond when he broke his reverie and tuned to the possible dangers and purpose of his running. The moon was now totally obscured and the street was over a hundred feet away, so that whatever light from streetlamps filtered through the trees was diluted to virtually nothing.

He chided himself for concentrating on the possible dangers from his friends in the Cadillac to the extent that he ignored the real dangers of tripping in the dark or twisting an ankle. That wouldn't do. He slowed his pace.

The road started to bend toward the street and he should be coming soon to the tree where Nancy was to wait. He hoped he could pick it out.

Something nudged his arm and scratched at his face. He swallowed a small yelp as he saw that it was a small shrub jutting out. He had almost run into it. Where was the moon?

Now the road and the outside street were converging fast and the pond was down to his left. Nancy should be just ahead. He had to leave the road and climb a small grassy embankment to the fence. The ground was knobby with roots and clumps and he broke to a walk.

He checked the street. He was at the right spot but there was no sign of Nancy. That was okay. They hadn't synchronized watches over this. She was probably hung up in traffic. He'd finish the loop and check again when he came back.

Where the road looped around the pond gave him the most apprehension. It was at its narrowest and he would be at his most vulnerable because escape to either side was cut off by the pond itself to the left and the fence and tangled shrubs to the right.

For a moment, he considered avoiding it, cutting across behind it and picking up the circumference road on the other side. But Alison, when she had run, had no doubt gone around the pond because that was her and Doug's regular route. He should follow her route.

The moon came back out and glinted off the pond. It was frozen almost out to the center although the ice didn't appear too thick. When he crossed the little cement bridge, the road swung sharply to the left and inclined steeply. Peter enjoyed hills and this one was a good challenge, running up a quarter mile at least.

At the crest of the hill, the road ran straight for a long stretch, and the cemetery, to his left, undulated down, bowl-like, to its center, a huge scoop of vague, dark shapes and outlines. But so far Peter had seen or heard nothing untoward. He wondered whether kids came in here to drink, carouse, or vandalize. They must. It was a common problem. If any were here, they could be a threat and he must be alert to that possibility.

He recognized the looming figure of the Union soldier near the Beauchesne and Carmichael grave sites. Could there be a logical, legitimate reason for that grave that had been tampered with? Maybe he should come back in the day, look for others, compile a list, and present it to Lieutenant Gabriel.

Abruptly, the moon went back behind a cloud and the darkness thickened but by now Peter's eyes had adjusted and he could still see fairly well. Certainly well enough not to run off the road into a tree.

He laughed as he thought of Paul Harrington, a running friend he had taught with, who once crashed into a telephone pole while running with his eyes closed. It was the sort of silly thing you sometimes do to amuse yourself when running, like seeing how far you can go holding your breath. Paul was trying to see if he could keep his eyes shut for a count of twenty. The road was wide and deserted and he thought he'd have no trouble. He had counted nineteen when he hit the pole dead center and stood dazed. Luckily, he hadn't knocked himself out, as the temperature had been about five degrees. It had been a dumb thing to do, but any dumber than this? Peter wondered. The remarkable thing was that Paul had admitted to it all.

Something clattered past Peter, rocketing into the shrubs.

"Jesus." Whirling, Peter raised his arms protectively before venting a nervous, high laugh. It was probably a pheasant or other large bird. The cemetery was reputed to have game birds. It took several seconds before he could no longer feel his pulse in his throat.

The moon re-emerged and he picked up his pace. The road turned to the left again and he was on the stretch leading back to the main entrance. As he approached it, he could see the Jaguar through the fence beneath the streetlamp. There were no other cars. The open area and rotary by the caretaker's cabin, dappled in moonlight, seemed clear and he scooted past. He had completed one lap. He tried to read his watch, couldn't make it out, and dismissed the time, because of stopping by the fence and varying his speed, as invalid anyway.

As he made the decline by the pond again, taillights glowed by the rendezvous tree and he recognized them as the Monza's.

He scuffed up the embankment to the fence and with a little difficulty shimmied to the top, raised himself over the spikes, and dropped to the other side. The damn thing had to be seven feet high.

Nancy had her window down, watchful for him. As he approached, she leaned over and unlocked the passenger's door.

"Well?" she asked, anticipatory, as he got in.

"Nothing. I saw nothing."

Carmine worked the wad of bubblegum exceptionally hard, blowing a rapid series of small bubbles, breaking each with a soft snap. When a yew branch brushed his face, he swore and yanked it aside. The crescent moon, a pale banana, didn't give nearly enough light to suit him.

What the hell was this teacher doing in here? You could have knocked Carmine over when the Jaguar drove to the cemetery. It was a good thing the Little Angel had decided to keep a tail on him. It would be a better thing when they decided to kiss him goodbye. Carmine stopped snapping bubbles long enough to smile as he thought of that.

The teacher had been easy as hell to follow. Didn't take any evasive maneuvers at all, not that they would have done him any good. When they had hit Oak Way Avenue, he simply doused his lights and stayed well behind, and when the Jaguar stopped near the main entrance to the cemetery, he and Louie had pulled into a side street and cut over about four blocks to the shadows of another side street that made a good observation point.

"Christ, he's going running," Louie said as Peter got out of his car.

"Maybe."

"What do you mean, maybe? He's got running stuff on. What the hell else is he going to do?"

Carmine worked his gum a moment before replying. Sometimes he couldn't believe how stupid Louie could be. "Louie, do you know what a coincidence is?"

Louie looked at Carmine hard. "Yeah, I know what a coincidence is. What do you think, I'm stupid?"

"Don't it seem funny that this bastard would come out *here* to run? I mean, after the nosing around he's been doing?"

Louie shrugged.

"I mean, how many people run in a cemetery at night? I sure as hell wouldn't."

Louie grinned. "What, are you afraid or something?"

"What, are you afraid or something?" Carmine mimicked. He watched Peter disappear through the side gate. He knew he had to check out what Peter was up to. He'd like to send Louie but the dumb bastard would screw it up, so he'd have to go himself.

"So, what are we going to do?"

"We'll give him a few minutes, then I'll go see what he's up to. You stay with the car."

Louie said nothing. That was fine with him. He didn't feel like poking around a cemetery at night.

After a few minutes, Carmine got out of the car and slipped across to the cemetery. When he got to the path of pine needles, he withdrew the magnum from his belt holster and cautiously advanced to the rotary. Unconsciously, he began rapid, soft poppings with his gum.

He stopped in the cover of a rhododendron before stepping into the open. There was no sign of Peter and he knew he had to operate on the assumption that he wasn't running. Christ, he couldn't be. What reason would he have to come running here at night?

First, Carmine checked the caretaker's cabin. The front door was locked and he went all around it, checking each window. Everything was tight. His eyes swept the bushes and the small open area between the cabin and the greenhouse. A low cement wall ran beside the greenhouse and he checked behind that too.

Next, he would check the chapel, about two hundred yards behind and to the left of the cottage. As he walked to it, a cloud blocked the moon, dropping the road, well away from the lamps of the outside street, into an even deeper darkness. Carmine checked behind him and to the sides, turning his body quickly and squinting to see better. He pointed the magnum back and forth and worked his gum rapidly.

This place was creepy as a bastard at night. Like something out of one of those horror movies. You had to give that guy credit for coming in here. It took guts. He thought of Louie sitting back in the Caddy and swore. He felt like slapping the stupid jerk around and maybe he would when he got back.

The chapel had its own greenhouse and Carmine checked the door to that first. It was secure but he peered inside at the oasis of fronds and ferns. Someone could hide in there pretty easily but they didn't get in through this door. There were two entrances to the chapel itself, plus the elevator entrance leading to the cellar, which could be opened only from the inside.

Geez, they had a good thing going here. Damn near perfect. The Little Angel was a slick son of a bitch to think of it. He had imagination and someday, Carmine promised himself, he'd get out of what he was doing and rise closer to the top, closer to the Little Angel. He wouldn't always be stuck working with a thick shit like Louie.

But first things first. Right now the thing was to do the best at what the Little Angel told you to do. And that was to keep an eye on this ex-teacher.

Carmine tried both entrances to the chapel and when satisfied they were locked stood a moment thinking. Should he make sure the teacher wasn't messing around any graves that had been reopened? But he wasn't really sure which ones had been reopened and to tell the truth didn't especially feel like penetrating any deeper into the cemetery. The hell with it. He'd go back and wait with Louie.

As he came back to the rotary, through the bushes he could see a shadow bobbing along the road to the right. He flopped his huge body into a hollow beside a towering linden tree, a black, gnarled silhouette against the re-emerged moon. He covered the gun so that it wouldn't gleam and froze his teeth on the wad of bubblegum.

Peter rounded the little curve and bounced past Carmine no more than ten feet away. Carmine watched him run past the cottage and disappear into the gloom. Crazy bastard. The son of a bitch *was* actually just running. Well, running, but maybe not *just* running. No. There were no maybes about it. He wasn't just running.

He got up, put the piece back in its holster, and went back out to wait with Louie. He wouldn't tell Louie that all he had seen was the teacher running. Louie would gloat.

In a few minutes the Monza drove up and Peter got out and went to the Jaguar.

"Who's that, the broad?" Louie said.

"Yeah."

"Nice piece. But what the hell is she doing here? What the hell is going on?"

Carmine stared at the Monza. Yeah, what the hell was going on? The teacher was up to something. Exactly what, Carmine wasn't sure. He had some ideas and wished he had someone besides Louie to sound them out on. Anyway, he'd get the word back to the Little Angel about this. He should find it very interesting.

CHAPTER 15

The phone rang.

"Damn," Peter said.

"Let it ring," Nancy said.

Peter waited through five more rings before rolling away from Nancy and reaching for the phone beside his bed.

It was Doug Symonds.

"Sorry to bother you, Peter. Are you busy?"

"Yeah, I'm straight out here, Doug, but I can use the break." Peter winked at Nancy, who shook her head at the pun. Then Peter felt guilty about joking behind Doug's back.

"Want me to call back?"

"No, really, no problem, Doug. What's up?"

"I won't hold you. I just felt like talking, so I called."

"I'm glad you did." Peter slid back into the warmth of the bedcovers. Nancy cuddled up to him. Peter waited for Doug to broach the topic of Alison and the thought of it wilted his passion.

"Still nothing on Alison," Doug said. "I'm beginning to think there never will be."

Peter groped for something innocuous to say that wouldn't reveal agreement with Doug's pessimism. Unsuccessful, he took a different tack. "Doug, how about coming over again for a few beers, a sandwich. Nothing fancy. What do you say?"

"No, no. Why I called was to see if some night we could go out for a few beers, though, if you don't mind."

"Sure. Let's do that. You name it."

"I'm free tomorrow night, if you are."

"That sounds good. Meet me here. What time, about eight? And we'll shoot out somewhere for a few pops."

After he hung up, Peter lay back on the pillow, Nancy's head on his chest.

"So Doug needs an ear again, huh?" she said.

"Can't blame him. He sounded pretty resigned to the worst."

"You're not going to tell him about, you know, what you've found out since?"

"Hell no. That would confirm it."

They lay a few minutes with their thoughts, listening to the background stereo.

"We've got company," Nancy said as Clark pounced on the bed, immediately beginning his kneading and purring. "What is he, a voyeur?"

"We're not doing anything."

"I know." She kissed the soft spot in his throat. "Maybe he's hopeful."

Clark moved up closer to the pillow, his kneading and purring intensifying.

"God, he sounds like a damn motorboat. Do you put up with this every night?"

"Man is not meant to sleep alone." When she gave him a mock strange look, he added, "Actually, he usually sleeps on the sofa."

Nancy sat up and reached over for a cigarette. Clark nudged her hands with his head as she lit it. As she sank back down, blowing a stream of smoke, she gave in and scratched his ears.

"You're not going to let talking to Doug get you started again, are you?"

"What do you mean?"

"You know damn well what I mean. Last night we agreed that you had done all you could short of going into the cemetery with a shovel, that you would let this rest. You did your bit, you ran in the damn place, nearly gave me heart failure waiting for you, and found nothing."

"I thought you were finding it exciting, an adventure, a chance to give play to your Nancy Drew fantasies."

She rolled her eyes. "The man is a nut, Clark, did you know that? You live with a lunatic."

She puffed on her cigarette. "Peter, I hate to strike the sour note, but the way I figure it, it is simple. Either Alison has gone off on her own, in which case there is nothing we can do. Or she has . . . well, you know. What I'm saying is that she is not being kept prisoner someplace like in a Gothic novel. People don't do that today. So, you have come to the dead end."

"Right you are, Nancy. We have discussed this *ad nauseam* and I agree." His light tone did not reflect his heavy feelings.

"You promise?"

"I promise."

She looked skeptical. "A man is as good as his word."

"I'll be true to mine."

She crushed out her cigarette, gave Clark a nudge to the floor, and rolled in to Peter.

"Now, let's see, where were we when the phone rang?"

CHAPTER 16

George DiLisio washed the mouthful of fettuccine down with a swallow of inexpensive California burgundy. The short, white-haired man across from him had nearly finished his own plate but still had almost a full glass of wine. It was his second. When he finished that, they could talk business. During the meal, however, conversation was confined to things like weather, sports not related to gambling (which meant practically none), or international politics. In other words, anything that couldn't be controlled and predicted and thus easily translated into money through gaming.

How many years had George and his boss, Milano Corso, the Little Angel, been having lunch in this upstairs room, reserved for just them, over Maria's restaurant? A long time. A time of mutual trust and respect. George broke off a piece of bread from the loaf in the basket, buttered it, and looked out and down onto Hanover Street, thick with midday traffic and commerce. Yes, he had eaten here a long time and stared out the window at the North End with this man who had controlled Boston and for the last few years all of New England.

The Little Angel. Supposedly the title went back to when Milano was ten and was brought home in a police cruiser for beating a boy two years older and setting his dog on fire. Mrs. Corso had thrown her hands up and exclaimed that the police must be mistaken, that her little angel wouldn't do something like that. The story had gotten around and the name had stuck. But no one referred to him as that in his presence.

The Little Angel sipped his wine, patted his lips, and smiled across the table. "This is good wine. Remember it.

Maybe we should write it down." The Little Angel liked wine but experimented only in the inexpensive.

"I already did remember it. We've had it before. I think maybe in the fall, in October sometime."

The Little Angel cocked his head and looked surprised. He lifted his glass and studied the deep red liquid. "It's very good. Funny that I don't remember it. You sure?"

"I'm sure. Don't you remember we liked it so much that Maria said she'd put a few bottles aside for us. You can't get it anymore. They don't make it."

As he chewed, the Little Angel struck a pensive pose, trying to recall. He smiled again, revealing good teeth. "Yes, I remember now. It was around Columbus Day." Then he shook his head. "You say they don't make it anymore? That's a shame."

Eating and sipping in silence, they finished their meal. The Little Angel pushed his plate aside and slid his chair back, a signal that the meal was over. Perhaps one transition and they could talk business. George reached into his suit coat for a cigarette and lit it. The Little Angel did not smoke.

"Ah, that Maria, how she can cook, eh? She should get a prize."

George nodded vigorous assent. He was anxious to talk but knew better than to rush it. The last thing the Little Angel wanted was a yes man but that didn't mean that George could ignore protocol.

Leaning back in his seat, he puffed contentedly, appraised his empty plate with the demeanor of one savoring again, in his mind, the meal he had just eaten, and shifted his glance around the little room set up in homey fashion by Maria, replete with curtains, pictures, and even fresh flowers.

"So tell me, what's bothering you?" the Little Angel said.

George was only momentarily startled at having his mood so easily read. The Little Angel had an uncanny ability to penetrate the thoughts of other people, an ability that was no small factor in his success and survival.

George smiled. "What makes you think something is bothering me?" He blew smoke at the ceiling, pushed his chair back, and crossed his legs, ankle on knee. "Actually, nothing is bothering me. I'm just wondering about—"

"Let me guess," the Little Angel interrupted. "It's the matter of speculation, my friend, is it not?"

George made an expression of assent: a slight nod, a quick, small smile.

"Tell me, your objections, are they still the same?"

"They are pretty much the same. I think it is unnecessary and that it involves risk, unnecessary risk."

The Little Angel smiled. He respected George's opinion, valued him as a foil for his own views, although in this instance they had been through this before. "You are right. On both counts. This speculation isn't really necessary. We can do quite well without it. And we *are*. But there's enough stuff available to us that by putting aside some on speculation we don't really cut into current profits."

The Little Angel had a momentary urge for a canoli but quickly pushed it aside. He wagged a ringed finger at George. "I've said it before and I'll say it again, we never know when the political climate will cut down traffic. Maybe never, but if it happens we'll have something to fall back on. And, as far as I know, we'll be the only ones. And, my good friend, can you imagine the price we can command if that should happen?"

George smiled, more from politeness than agreement, at the rhetorical question.

"As for risk . . ." The Little Angel shrugged. "There's always risk. It doesn't worry me especially. The tie-in to us is indirect. At worst, we might lose some material." He shrugged again. "Actually, I think the whole deal we've got going has worked out very well. It's taken care of a few problems."

George nodded, thoughtful. "Michael spoke to me this morning. Carmine reported to him that this Swann guy went out to the cemetery last night."

"And?"

"He jogged, for chrissakes. But Carmine says he thinks the guy is looking around."

The Little Angel made an expression of distaste. "Carmine is a fool. Is he the best we can do?"

"We can always bring in someone, but for routine stuff, I think he's pretty reliable. He's got a point. It is unusual to go jogging there at night."

"Perhaps."

George shifted ankle on knee. "Carmine says Swann drove out alone in his car but that his girl came out later and picked him up in hers at some place and drove him back to his car." He sucked on his cigarette. "That is strange. Carmine thinks he is going to be trouble and should be taken care of."

"Carmine is too quick. He needs someone to check him. That business with the Stella kid was not handled well at all."

George felt a moment's pique. This was a disturbing flaw in the Little Angel, that if something did not turn out well to place blame in the execution of the order rather than in the order itself. "He did what he was told."

The Little Angel appeared to be brooding. "Make sure he continues to do as he is told, which for now is to just keep an eye on Swann."

George nodded but said, "I think Carmine is right. I think Swann is trouble. Too much sticking his goddam nose in where it doesn't belong."

The Little Angel pursed his lips. "What do you recommend?"

George made a decisive chopping motion with his hand.

The Little Angel looked evenly at his friend and then looked out the window to the roofs of Boston's North End, some of them unchanged since Paul Revere lived there.

"No," he finally said. "He still just keeps a watch." He turned from the window and looked directly at his friend. "See to it that Carmine gets the word on that. Hands off."

The Little Angel looked back out the window. Again, he

buried the desire for a canoli. The sky was the even, listless gray that signaled a likely snowfall.

George thought that the matter was over when the Little Angel, still staring out, said, "Unless, of course, Swann goes back out to the cemetery. If he does, Carmine knows what to do."

CHAPTER 17

It had snowed about four inches the previous night. Peter
scuffed by the State House, down by the Common, past the
Park Street Church, under the big steaming kettle by the
corner coffee shop, to City Hall. The bricks on the plaza had
been cleared and were stained with salt.

He pushed through the revolving doors into the main lobby
and the clutter of people on the various political businesses of
admonishing, importuning, compromising, or just gawking. At
this hour, there weren't many gawkers. The tourists would
come later, drifting over from Quincy Market.

In one corner was an information stand. He went to it,
asked directions of the burly, pleasant black man, and walked
to one of the elevators. He pushed the "up" button and stared
back out at the lobby. This was his first time in City Hall and
he couldn't decide whether he liked it. It had received raves
for its architecture when it was built, but to Peter it looked
rather like an upside-down pyramid whose peak had been
buried deep in brick and asphalt. The lobby looked like something from an old M-G-M Roman extravaganza. Peter imagined the mayor and City Council in togas slowly descending
the stairs.

He went up to the eighth floor, to room 816, City Parks and
Recreation. He had to wait almost five minutes for the girl at
the phones to acknowledge him. She doodled, fiddled with
her curly perm, and said "yeah" into the phone eleven times
after he started counting. At his sign of impatience, she signaled with a finger that she was almost through. She said
"yeah" three more times, "bye-bye," and hung up.

"Yes, sir?" She smiled at him, a recompense for his having to wait.

"Morning. I'm interested in getting general information on city-run cemeteries."

She looked blankly at him and fiddled with her perm. Two lights glowed on the phone. She looked at them but did not pick up the receiver. "What kind of information?"

"I'm not sure. History, size, number of workers. Maybe even a map or diagram. That sort of thing."

A third light glowed and she fiddled some more. "Like, do you have any particular cemetery in mind?"

Peter watched one of the lights go out. "Not really." He wondered whether this evasion was worth it. "Just the bigger ones. You know, maybe like Oak Way, for example."

The girl got up. "Wait a minute."

Peter appraised her as she walked into another room. He glanced around. All the walls were plain poured concrete, the furniture, here at least, contemporary. The starkness was broken by abundant large potted plants. The whole place looked as though it should be cold, but it wasn't.

The girl came back out, smiling, still atoning for the phone delay. "I'm sorry, sir, but we don't have that kind of information here." She sat at her desk and ripped off a piece of paper from a pad. "But all that information is kept out at Woodlawn Cemetery," she said, writing on the paper and then handing it to him. "If you'll see Tom Doyle out there, he'll be glad to help you."

Peter looked at the name she had written on the back of a While You Were Out slip.

"As a matter of fact, if you want," she said, still smiling and toying with a tight curl over her right ear, "I can call ahead and see if he is in now and tell him you're coming."

Peter smiled back. "No, don't bother, thank you. I don't know exactly when I'll get out there."

She nodded, smiled even more broadly, a warm, helpful-public-servant smile, and answered the phone as Peter left.

Woodlawn was in Jamaica Plain and Peter drove with some disquiet. If he was still being watched, going to City Hall was one thing; going to Woodlawn was another. At City Hall, his business could be almost anything, but going out to *any* cemetery at this point looked strange.

His conscience also pricked him somewhat. He had promised Nancy he would drop the matter, but since last night's talk with Doug his need to know had been revived. After all, he told himself, implied in the promise was that he would drop the matter because he had come to a stone wall, a dead end. But now, once again, he wasn't sure he had come to a dead end. Maybe there was something about the cemetery—its layout, perhaps; or who worked there—that would give him an insight about the fates of Ricky Scalise, Tommy Stella, and Alison Bradley.

The sun sliced through the breaking overcast and the wind had picked up from the northwest, dropping the temperature to the teens. Road-salt spray from traffic splotched the windshield. The Jaguar's windshield washer had long ago retired and Peter knew that if he worked the wipers he would have a hopeless smear. By the time he reached the cemetery, the windshield situation bordered on hazardous.

Inside the cemetery, he had to drive a short way to the caretaker's office. He parked in the small parking area, reached under his seat for a rag, and wiped off his windshield as he observed all around him. The wind slithered through his jacket and numbed his bare fingers. Especially, he checked back where he had come in to see whether he was being followed. He conceded that he was an amateur in such matters and that he would know neither how to spot a tail nor how to lose one.

If he was being tailed, would they check in here after he left to see what he had been up to? Quite likely they would, he thought. No. They would be *certain* to. Or possibly more than just Oak Way Cemetery was involved in whatever this whole mess was all about. Maybe the Tom Doyle he was going to see at this cemetery would immediately transfer word back about his inquiries.

These were real risks. Peter felt a moment's frustration. He felt there was absolutely no question that he had stumbled onto something very wrong, but he could do nothing to prove it or even to get the police officially interested. By his persistence, he knew he was jeopardizing himself, yet he wondered how much more there was that he didn't know about. Logic said there had to be more. Much more. It was inconceivable, against the laws of probability, that any wrongdoing at Oak Way Cemetery was confined to just three people that he, a floating free agent, would hear about.

He put the rag back in the car and went to the office. Inside, he had to wait a few minutes for Tom Doyle. A woman at an old wooden desk struggled with an equally old typewriter. Manicured nails wouldn't make it here. She told him that Tom Doyle was out supervising a gravedigging but should be right back and would he care to sit and wait?

Peter sat in the only other chair in the office besides the secretary's. There was nothing to read and no music.

The woman, late forties, he pegged her, pleasant-looking, caught his eye and smiled. He smiled back.

"It's getting colder, isn't it?"

"Yes."

She pursed her lips and shook her head grimly as if this outrage of the weather was something new to winter. Peter sensed that she wasn't finished and that comments on last night's snowfall were coming next. He hated small talk about the weather and chided himself on that snobbery. He knew its purpose. Like tail wagging in dogs, it said: We're friendly; we won't go for each other's throats. We'll discuss something noncontroversial, something mutually agreeable. He resolved he would even add to the conversation, keep the ball rolling.

The door opened and a thin man who looked close to retirement with wispy gray hair stepped in and spared Peter from having to cope with commentary about the wind-chill factor.

"Ah, here's Mr. Doyle now," the secretary said.

Peter stood and extended his hand. Tom Doyle grasped it firmly and cocked his head inquisitively. Peter explained his business and was led into another room beyond the old desk.

"Sure," said Tom Doyle affably, "we've got that stuff back in here somewhere."

Peter evaluated Doyle's manner for a sinister sign or an indication that he was acting guarded but could detect nothing. Tom Doyle seemed to want to be helpful, seemed pleased to be able to offer information about something that probably few ever inquired about.

"Let's see, Oak Way, you say. Should be right here." He went to a tall file cabinet behind a desk and opened the bottom drawer. He fiddled for a moment, reached into his pocket for glasses, and pulled out a folder, dust testifying to its long undisturbed rest.

"Oak Way's not the oldest in the city by a long shot, but still you've got burials going back to the early seventeen-hundreds." He laid the folder on the desk and opened it, peering over his glasses.

"What do you want this stuff for? You a writer? Seems like the kind of stuff a writer would be interested in."

"Yes," Peter said, "I'm doing a little writing on the cemeteries of Boston."

"Oh? The *Globe*? *Herald*?"

"I'm free-lance. I don't know just yet where I'll use this."

Tom Doyle nodded. "Never could write. Like to read but never *could* write worth a damn. Don't know how you do it." He took off his glasses. "Well, help yourself. I've got to get back out. You can sit here and look. Right here is where you'll find the most on the subject. Maybe find a little more at the BPL too. When you're done, just leave it here. Mrs. Conway will put it away."

Tom Doyle stuck out his hand. "Let me know when your article is coming out. I'd like to read it."

Peter shook hands again, nodded, and assured him that he would do that.

The folder contained a map of Oak Way Cemetery and

loose, numbered sheets of information, the sort of thing that Peter had anticipated. Oak Way was first used in 1703 and gradually expanded. Peter noted with interest that at one point it was a pauper's graveyard and that several British and American casualties of Bunker Hill were buried there.

On another sheet were estimates that within ten years all plots would be taken and recommendations were for better utilization of space by conversion to mausoleums. According to the sheet, objections to that had been raised by citizens in the neighborhoods abutting the cemetery who feared that construction of mausoleums would lead to the destruction of the cemetery's exotic trees and shrubs. Apparently, they saw Oak Way as more a public park than a cemetery.

Peter put the sheet aside. He could see nothing in it that related to what he was looking for. What *am* I looking for? he wondered.

Next, he spread the map on the desk and studied it. In one corner was listed random statistical information. The cemetery was 134 acres and the perimeter road that he had run looped for 1.6 miles.

His glance skipped across the map. The caretaker's cottage, the greenhouse, the chapel were all labeled, as were the paths and streets. He started to fold the map when something caught his eye. He stared at it and felt his pulse quicken. Pushing the map aside, he pulled out the remaining sheets and scanned them, knowing he was closing in.

Then he found it. He stared for a long moment at the piece of miscellaneous information that explained so much but still left so much unanswered. Oak Way Cemetery had a crematorium.

Carefully, he returned everything to the folder and thanked Mrs. Conway as he walked out back to his car. He started the engine and abstractedly watched the tachometer needle bounce up and then settle on 900. He wondered what to do next. What he had found pushed the stone wall, the dead end, back even further.

Now he was certain of what had happened to Alison Bradley. But he didn't know why. He shuddered as he thought of it. But his fear was not nearly as strong as his outrage.

Carmine picked the girl up in the Combat Zone. He had had her many times before and she liked to think their relationship went at least a little beyond money paid for services rendered.

It was late and they were both "off duty." She said she wanted some Chinese food and he, being tired and hungry, agreed. It was the proverbial stone's throw from the Combat Zone to Chinatown. Louie had taken the car, so they walked, not arm in arm, but at least side by side—a hulking man whose size and body language registered "stay away" to any would-be muggers, and the girl, long ago a woman, actually, whose demeanor and body language registered instantly what she was.

"Come on, in here," she said, indicating a small place with Chinese lettering all over it. He hesitated. He didn't like small places. They made him nervous, made him feel trapped.

"Come on," she said again.

They went in. The man behind the cash register was about to tell them it was too late to seat them, that the kitchen was ready to close, but a quick assessment of Carmine changed his mind.

Sitting, they studied their menus, she smiling, pleased with this courtship-like aspect of the evening; he scowling, puzzled by the diversity of the menu. Carmine was no connoisseur, but while he was insensitive to quality, he enjoyed quantity. He ate a lot.

"What do you want?" she asked. Her name was Shirley.

He made a noncommittal gesture. "You order. Just make sure you get enough. I'm hungry."

She ordered the combination dinner for four and a Zombie for herself. Carmine got a bottle of Bud to start.

"Wait'll you try the spareribs here," Shirley said, reaching across and touching his hand, a paw the size of a child's catcher's mitt.

He grunted and withdrew the paw. He was in a bad mood. He was getting tired of following this ex-teacher in the Jaguar and more than irritated by the orders which had come down to keep his hands off unless the guy went back out to Oak Way. Christ, it was clear as hell that Swann was nosing around where he shouldn't be.

What the hell did the Little Angel want, for him to blow the lid off the whole deal? Maybe the Little Angel was starting to go soft upstairs. Maybe it was time for a change, but Carmine knew it wasn't for him to suggest it. Better not to let anyone even know he was thinking it. That would be suicide.

He wondered for a moment who they would get if they ever put a contract on himself. Would it be Louie? No way. Louie was dangerous and would do what he was told and for sure didn't feel any loyalty or bonds of friendship for Carmine, but he was too goddam stupid. Probably, they'd bring in someone from New York or Cleveland.

He dismissed the train of thought and considered Peter Swann's actions this morning. Going out to Woodlawn Cemetery had really baffled Carmine. There had to be a connection between that and this sniffing around Oak Way unless the dude had a thing for stiffs.

He probably should report it but he'd take his time. Let them know about it tomorrow. The hell with them, the Little Angel and the others. He'd already warned them. He wouldn't bust his ass running up with every little thing that this Swann guy did.

Still, it was goddam strange. He probably should have checked in at Woodlawn to see what Swann had wanted. But he hadn't done that either. Maybe he'd do that tomorrow. Have Louie tail him alone—he could do that at least—while he found out what Swann had been checking on.

Carmine finished his Bud in one gulp from the bottle and looked around for the waiter to get him another but the food was already on its way. One thing about the Chinks, he thought; you didn't have to wait for your chow.

He ordered another beer and Shirley wanted another Zombie. He piled his plate high with a lot of everything: ribs, wings, noodles, rice, and other things he couldn't identify.

"Geez, you're a classy guy," Shirley said after he helped himself and pushed the food her way. He didn't smile and his look made her regret the comment.

They chewed in silence and when he looked at her his irritation increased. Dumb slut chewed with her mouth open.

He finished his plate quickly and dipped in for more. He had nearly cleaned everything out when he asked her if she wanted anything else.

"Yeah, how about saving me a couple ribs at least. Good thing we got dinner for four."

"Told you I was hungry." He burped slightly, washed down a mouthful with his second Bud and signaled for another. "Want another one of those?" he said, nodding at her Zombie.

She smiled and tried to look arch. "I'd better not or I'll be no good for anything else, know what I mean?"

He regarded her without lust or humor. She had something on her teeth, maybe rice. "You might as well get another drink."

She dropped her smile. "What about after?"

"Forget it. I'm tired."

Leaning back in her seat, she sneered. "Well, la di da, aren't you the big stud. A couple of beers and you're wiped out."

Carmine reached across, grabbing her arm, and pulled her forward, nearly tipping the table. "Listen, you cheap little bitch, don't get cute with me."

Shoving her back, he stood up and looked around for his waiter, who, with the others, was trying to look inconspicuous. Carmine, his hunger now satisfied, wanted to sleep, to forget his anger at having to be up early to spend another day following Swann. How much longer would this stupid tailing continue? Maybe he'd get lucky and Swann would go back to Oak Way. He almost smiled at that.

He took a bill from his wallet, slapped it on the table, and turned to leave. Halfway to the door, he looked back at the sulking Shirley and said, "Why don't you go home and try brushing your teeth?"

CHAPTER 18

Peter sat in the Jaguar near the T station across from the sprawling General Electric plant in Lynn. It was just after seven, no sign yet of the morning sun through the low overcast, and the wind sliced through the nine-degree temperature. He wished that he had borrowed Nancy's car but he hadn't wanted to give her any indication that he was checking things out again.

He took off his glove and felt by the heater. The best he could say for the air it spewed was that it wasn't out-and-out cold.

He watched the traffic cop ready himself for the rush of cars that would signal the end of the eleven-to-seven shift. Reluctantly, he gave up the comfort of his cruiser and positioned himself across from the gateway by the enormous parking lot.

Peter sat forward as the flow started and when he spotted the old blue Maverick that leaned to one side he beeped his horn and waved.

At first he thought he hadn't been seen, but then the Maverick pulled over. He got out and ran up to it. The door sagged when opened, caught stuck on something, and popped and grated when he pulled it wide. He climbed in and sat on a blown-out seat.

"What the *hell* you doing out here, Peter?" Joey Blowtorch asked.

Peter wasted no time on amenities. It was obvious that Joey wasn't thrilled to see him. "Joey, I know what they did to Ricky Scalise and Tommy Stella."

Joey looked at Peter incredulously. He shook his head. "Yeah, so do I and everyone else. They killed them."

"Yeah. But I mean I know *how*. I know what's been going on. Some of it anyway."

"I'm not interested." Joey looked straight ahead as if inspecting the religious statue on the dashboard.

"Joey, listen to me a minute. I know you think I should keep out of this, but there's something I've got to tell you."

He told Joey about Alison.

Joey checked his rearview mirror, swiveled in his seat, looked about nervously, and then turned to Peter exasperated. "Peter, what are you telling *me* all this for?"

"I know how and *why* Ricky and Tommy got it. I know *how* Alison Bradley got it. But I can't figure *why*. At least not specifically. I figure she saw something she wasn't supposed to. That much seems obvious."

Peter adjusted himself on the seat. A spring threatened to pop through. "To help me find out exactly what she might have seen, I need some help from you."

"Peter, get out of the car."

"Joey, wait, please. Just a little help."

"I'm afraid to ask."

"I have to pull a little B and E."

"Where?"

"At Oak Way Cemetery. That's where all three got it. I want to get into the chapel out there. I don't know how to do it, at least with any delicacy. You're the expert on that kind of thing."

Joey stared at Peter, looked at the statue, and stared back at Peter. "You are a lunatic. You know that? You are a goddarn lunatic."

Peter pressed. "I was hoping to get you to come out with me. If not, then at least tell me what I need and how to go about breaking into a place without having to use a fire ax."

The Maverick's heater was beginning to blow hot air already. Not exotic, no image, it leaned, but it was warm.

Joey ran his hand through his hair. He looked tired. "Peter, we've been friends how long? I give you some friendly advice which you chose to ignore. That's okay. That's your business. But now you are trying to get me involved. Get me maybe killed along with you."

"We've been friends a *long* time, Joey. That's why I came to you. And that's why I figure you'll tell me what I need to know and why you won't say anything about what I told you to anyone. Not to Sam. Not to Barbie. Not to anyone."

A few minutes later, Peter got out of the Maverick, then leaned back in and said, "Thanks much, Joey. Wish me luck."

Water and sky melded into one cold, gray, amorphous gel as the thirty-foot Wellcraft Scarab knifed along at thirty miles an hour. At the wheel, Bobby Pratt was cold and nervous. These cold-weather runs at seven-thirty in the morning weren't what he pictured when he had taken on this deal. Salem and Beverly Harbor in December wasn't exactly San Diego.

The slipstream buffeted and clawed at Bobby's hood and parka and the prickle of nervous sweat was a cold film between skin and thermal underwear. Besides the cold, the trouble this time of year was that practically no one else was out on the water and he knew he was conspicuous. During the good boating weather, not that long a season, there was so much traffic that the cops or the Coast Guard weren't too likely to single out any one particular boat.

Bobby laughed to himself. Actually, when you got down to it, there really wasn't a problem. The harbor masters went into hibernation in the winter anyway. Couldn't blame them. What the hell did he read that they made a year? Twelve grand? Fifteen grand? Something like that. Scato. And the nearest Coast Guard was in Boston, not that far by water or helicopter, but better than it must have been when they were perched right at the edge of Salem Harbor on Winter Island.

But Bobby really couldn't complain. Over the past three years, he had made five, maybe six, really cold-weather runs, although in April or May, even June sometimes, you could

freeze your ass off out here. The reason was, he'd heard somewhere, that north of the Cape is influenced by the Labrador
Current and south of it by the Gulf Stream.

But the dough was really good, well worth a few goose
pimples—for what? an hour or two's work all told a few times
a year. And he didn't have to go out and get involved in the
hassle of selling coke on the street.

The best part, the bonus, was the Scarab. What he had always wanted. She had a nice little cabin under that long
prow, could sleep four. Perfect for beer, buzzin', and broads.
And talk about handling. This baby with her two 455-cubic-
inch V-8s, each good for 370 horse, could do an honest seventy miles an hour. (No one said knots anymore, except the
old buzzards.)

Heads turned when she went by. Awesome. But you could
tell the guys with sails, the pipe smokers from Marblehead,
were really pissed. They'd like to give you the finger if they
weren't so goddam pure.

Bobby knew that using a rig like the Scarab was actually
sort of an anachronism for this kind of thing. Her speed really
wasn't an asset if they had a fix on you. A copter could follow
you till you tied up and alert the regular cops to be waiting.
The deal now was to blend in by having something ordinary-
looking, but Bobby didn't want to go that route and give up
the Scarab. So far there had never been any trouble, and if he
thought that he was going to be apprehended, his standing orders were to just dump the stuff. Open the package and spill
it. Give the fish a high.

Yeah, it was a good deal having an uncle with connections.
Uncle Sal, his widowed ma's brother, was like a father. He
took care of Ma and Bobby real well.

Bobby looked at his watch. He had to meet Uncle Sal in a
little over an hour at the Revere Drive-In. No sweat. As usual,
it had gone real smooth. He'd made his rendezvous about a
mile beyond Misery Island, picked up the package, and was
now almost back to Beverly Harbor Marina. The reduce-

speed sign was just ahead and he drew down on the throttles and brought her down to about eight miles an hour.

After he tied up, he'd zip up 128 to Route 1 in his 'Vette, also courtesy of Uncle Sal, and deliver the package. He wondered what its final street value would be. Coke was whacked five times before the user got it. Bobby estimated what this package weighed, did a little quick math in his head, and smiled to himself at the ball-park figure he came up with.

No wonder Uncle Sal could treat him well. He wondered when he could approach him about the possibility of what he *really* wanted: a Formula Thunderbird 402. Forty feet two inches. Twin Gale Banks Turbo-charged 600-horse 455s. Actually not as fast as the Scarab, but a better party boat. Bigger cabin with more stuff in it, even a shower and radar range, for chrissakes.

He killed the port engine and began the troll to his slip. No sign of cops or any unwelcome reception committee. He'd just slip the package in his backpack and scoot out to Revere. He had plenty of time to grab a coffee at McDonald's first too, which he really needed to warm up.

Also, he could think about whether he should ask Uncle Sal about the Formula Thunderbird. It was almost Christmas.

Peter stopped at a hardware store in Lynn and bought a disposable flashlight and a carpenter's crowbar. In addition to its function as a break-in tool, it could serve as a weapon. He had considered taking a knife this time, but the crowbar would serve nicely.

B and E wasn't necessarily as sophisticated as he had thought. His notion had been that you had to do tricky things with a credit card, but that wouldn't work on a dead bolt, Joey had told him.

He didn't know what kind of lock he would encounter on the chapel at Oak Way. He wished he could research that before actually going out to break in, but he didn't dare risk another observed trip out there. He told Joey that probably the door was old, heavy wood with perhaps one of those old-fashioned big-key locks.

Reluctantly, Joey had told him that if the lock was heavy, often you didn't even bother with it. With the crowbar, you simply pried back the frame around the door enough so that the latch bolt was free. Success in that depended, of course, on the nature of the doorframe but most of them had a half inch to an inch of give.

Easier than that was simply knocking the hinge pins free if the hinges were exterior, as they frequently were on old doors of the type the chapel probably had. Or he might luck out and be able to unscrew the lock itself. Finally, Joey had said, a good kick would sometimes do it, depending on the lock. If things got any more involved than these approaches, Joey had said, "Forget it, which is what you should do, anyway."

Peter drove back to Boston totally engrossed in his plans for going out to Oak Way Cemetery late that afternoon.

He was unaware of the black Cadillac following several car lengths behind.

Alex Harris made the pickup at 9 A.M. He had gotten the word the day before that a delivery would be made today. A day's notice was adequate for the necessary preparations.

The important thing, the tricky part, was picking a site for storing the stuff. An old grave was good because the chances were there would be no one coming around, family or friends, to notice that anything had been done. Problem there was that someone *could* notice and know that nothing *should* be happening there. But that was remote. No one ever really paid attention to that kind of thing.

A new grave, if one was available, was good because activity there—disturbed ground and all—was normal and accepted. But the timing was crucial. If you could, you moved in right away, right after the ceremony when everyone had cleared out and before the family might come back. They often did. For a week or two they were likely to pop back, the husband or wife, the son or daughter, at any time, and just stand around. So you didn't want anything amiss when that happened.

If you couldn't move right away, then the thing was to wait until night. No one came out at night except boozed-up kids sometimes, but they were easy to scare off. You just had to keep a careful watch for them.

Or that girl.

If you were going to work at night, you had to be sure the site was near the middle, away from the street. The way the cemetery dipped at its center made it so that from the street beyond the fence no one driving by would ever see anything.

A potential problem to be considered with a fresh site was the very remote possibility of an exhumation. If any strange circumstances surrounded the death that could lead to that, then that site had to be ruled out.

And finally, of course, was the problem of keeping tabs on everything. Records had to be kept but not where the wrong eyes would ever find them. Alex also had to give *them* a record of everything so that if anything happened to him they'd know where to find what they wanted.

But so far nothing had gone wrong. Oh, sure, the cops had come peeking around after that girl, but naturally they found nothing and never would. Important thing, though, was they appeared genuinely satisfied that nothing had happened to her at the cemetery.

Harold still bothered him somewhat. He was a strange one. You had to be strange to do what he did. Either strange to begin with or turned strange afterward. Burning bodies and pounding the skeletons to powder was not your usual occupation. Yeah, Harold had always been a creepy tight-lipped loner and was getting worse.

But the signs of strain he showed lately surprised Alex. All along, he had thought Harold would be the least affected of anyone because even though he was strange nothing seemed to bother him.

Today's job should go all right. A swap. Harold had never minded swaps. And this was some old lady who had lived to be ninety-three, so that shouldn't bother Harold any. And the family was unlikely to come messing around later. Her husband had died a year ago and the children, three daughters and a son, weren't too far from checking out themselves.

They would have been able to get everything done this morning except that Harold had a backlog of legitimate work scheduled for the day. That meant staying on after regular closing hours but they should be out of here by six-thirty, maybe seven at the outside.

Alex pulled in the main gate. It was almost quarter to ten. He stopped at the cottage, locked the truck, and checked in with Mary Sands, who had been here as long as he had. She was a good worker but ugly as sin. Alex smiled. If only she knew what was going on.

He told her he would be by the point gate at the beginning of Oak Way Avenue to wait for the funeral procession. That's how it worked. He'd wait in his truck and guide the lead car to the grave site. Then he and the others would discreetly disappear until the funeral was over.

In high spirits, Alex drove to the point gate, whistling something Christmasy. He touched the package on the seat beside him. Today's work would be a nice Christmas bonus. Damn nice.

Now, if only he could get Harold to snap out of it.

Peter wrapped a towel around the crowbar, securing it with heavy rubber bands. It was three-thirty and he would be leaving soon. He wanted to arrive after dark and to make sure that he wouldn't be followed. For some time he had wondered how to ensure that he wouldn't have a shadow. When the answer hit him, it was absurdly simple. He would run out. No car could travel the route a runner might take—sidewalks, alleys, one-way streets.

He admitted that he still wasn't certain what he was looking for. But he was hopeful of finding something. When he had gone to Woodlawn yesterday morning, he hadn't been certain then either, but had turned up the information that was sending him out now. That information, however, wasn't enough to *prove* anything. But he didn't know what he would find that might be proof, that the police could use to wrap this up. The police couldn't break and enter, but he could.

On impulse, he dialed the number Lieutenant Gabriel had given him, and when told Gabriel wasn't in, he hesitated and then said, "I'd like to leave a message, please. My name is Swann. Lieutenant Gabriel knows me. Tell him that I know what happened to Miss Bradley at Oak Way Cemetery but that I have no proof. I'm going out there now."

It was time to dress. He belted the toweled crowbar to his waist so that it ran along his side and partway down his hip over his thermal underwear. Next, he put on sweat shirt, sweat pants, and sweat jacket. The loose, bulky clothing would keep him warm and conceal the crowbar. The disposable flashlight fit securely in one sleeve and in the other he would hold a last-minute item—a small, slim Kodak Hawkeye Instamatic and a couple of flash cubes. Casey, Crime Photographer.

He looked outside. It would be fully dark when he arrived at Oak Way. It was a long run anyway, but his route might be circuitous both to elude pursuers, if any, and to avoid expressway traffic as much as possible. Also, he allowed that the crowbar would probably slow him considerably.

He breathed in deeply and slowly several times to quell the disquiet rising in him. Was it fear or excitement? He refused to get into self-analysis again; it could paralyze. He had committed himself to this and he would go now before he brought up the dozens of good reasons why he shouldn't.

He locked up and, without checking around, ran down Mount Vernon Street. He took a left at the bottom of the hill and headed for the Common. His plan was to loop randomly in the Common for about ten minutes, come out and cut across Charles to the Public Gardens, and then run down Commonwealth Avenue to Park Drive and the Jamaicaway.

By the time he hit Commonwealth Avenue, it was nearly dark. The camera and flashlight were behaving nicely but the crowbar was beginning to chafe and really restricted motion in his right leg. He was confident that he had eluded any shadow and decided against cutting up and down side streets as he originally planned. The hell with it.

He had no idea how long his searching could take at the cemetery and in the chapel itself, if, indeed, he could get in. Very possibly he would find nothing beyond what he already knew from the information gathered at Woodlawn and he would be out in minutes. On the other hand, things could lead to things and he might be there a while. Nancy had some kind of meeting tonight, she had told him, so there was no time commitment there.

As he crossed Hereford Street, running against traffic, a green Audi passing on the right swung past, nearly brushing him and forcing him between parked cars. He took that as an excuse to duck in the shadows a moment and adjust the crowbar. Then he was back out, trying to hit a decent stride.

By the time Peter had hit Oak Way Avenue, he had long since taken the crowbar from under his sweat shirt, deciding to carry it in his hand rather than risk ulceration of the hip and side. As he slipped through the gate, he quickly checked around and was satisfied that he had arrived unnoticed.

Instead of going directly to the chapel, he had decided to reconnoiter by doing one loop around first, knowing that just because he had seen nothing the other time he had run here at night didn't mean that he would again.

He kicked past the caretaker's cottage and began his loop. Beneath the sweat clothes, he was perspiring freely and felt chilled because his pace had not been rapid enough to maintain the body warmth that would normally offset the frigid air. He pulled his woolen cap away from his ears so that his hearing would be unobstructed.

It was beyond the halfway point, past the pond and back up the long incline, that he saw a flicker of light through the tangle of bare shrubbery to his left in the distance.

He stopped, stared, and listened. The air was calm and

frigid. Momentarily, he lost the light, back-stepped a bit and picked it up again, glimmering shakily down in the dip at the center of the cemetery. It was a flickering light, no doubt about that, and he wondered about it.

Cautiously, he jogged slowly toward it down a narrow, paved path, heavily overhung with bare, black, drooping arms of linden trees. The half-moon seared the snow cover and cast the jutting tombstones in stark relief. The path had been perfunctorily plowed and was splotched with smooth, white patches.

At the end of the path, he had to go left, around a wall of bare forsythia, the stripped whips of branches sticking up and then drooping in a clutter on the little road.

Peter stopped at the end of the wall of forsythia, in its cover. There were voices. Voices and other sounds. And what was that smell? He wrinkled his nose in distaste. It seemed to be coming from the other direction.

He peered around the bush. Perhaps sixty yards distant, he counted three men, a backhoe, and an old pickup truck. The men appeared to be putting the finishing touches on filling a grave. Two lanterns explained the flickering light.

Peter felt his pulse tick in his throat as he viewed the scene. This was dirty business of some sort, an illicit after-hours enterprise. Was this the kind of thing Alison had stumbled upon and had been discovered witnessing? He checked around him, hefting the crowbar high as he looked.

What the hell were they up to? Staying close to the bush, he stepped a little closer.

Alex Harris left Harold in the chapel and stepped outside, shaking his head. Jesus, sometimes you had to put a charge of dynamite under Harold to get him to move his ass. He would have been willing to sit there another hour or two just staring at the walls. He didn't even look at the girly magazines he had in the desk anymore. Alex thought about that and it worried him. He knew that it probably had to do with that girl . . .

Well, he didn't feel like waiting around here all night. There was no need of it. He had told Harold to get moving, and when he started to stammer protests that it was too soon to open the oven, Alex told him that was a load of bullshit. He reminded Harold how he used to boast that he could finish up, if he had to, after only an hour's wait.

Alex walked past the greenhouse and headed down to where the others were. They should be about done. He'd let them go when they were finished but he knew he'd have to hang around for Harold to get done. He sighed. It used to be that he could trust Harold to finish up on his own, but not lately. Christ, he was likely to do something, or forget to do something, that would screw things up.

It could be any little thing that could trip them up. Harold might leave lights on, leave the gate open, or some other trivial thing that could attract the cops. Or worse, he might get himself caught dumping the ashes.

Alex could just picture the cops coming by when everything had been done, and there were no traces, and checking on Harold because he had left a light on. He'd probably crack wide open and spill the beans when all he had to do was tell them the prearranged story they had rigged up for such an eventuality. After all, Harold was a legitimate worker here and could prove it but he'd probably get tongue-tied at first and then start screaming.

If it came to it, he'd do Harold's job himself, Alex thought. Really nothing to it, if you could stand it. But why not? When you got down to it, what was the big deal? He mulled that over. Maybe it was worth serious consideration. Harold was becoming a real weak link here. But what to do with him? Well, there *was* an answer to that. No one would ever miss Harold because, as far as Alex knew, practically no one knew he existed except his fellow workers.

Alex pulled his collar up. Jesus, it was cold. He almost started to whistle when he saw the figure bent forward behind the tall, bare shrubbery.

He stopped and shrank back against a tree trunk. Who the

hell was that? It wasn't a kid. He looked around for a large stone or something but the ground was snow-covered. He looked at the figure again and observed the running clothes and shoes. If whoever it was started to move away, he'd never catch him. Alex was no runner. He'd better move in right now.

Keeping as close to cover as he could, he moved in silently and quickly.

Carmine checked his watch, blew a big bubble, and swore under his breath. Where the hell was the teacher? His runs seldom took over an hour and this was the first time he had known him to be still running after dark except for that one time when he had run in the cemetery.

He and Louie were parked at the top of Mount Vernon, wedged in, as inconspicuously as possible, between other parked cars. Only one time had they tried to follow Peter when he had gone running, giving up when it became pointless and virtually impossible anyway.

"What's the matter?" Louie asked.

Carmine cast him a sideways glance. Louie was useless; he had nothing on the ball at all. Finally, he said, "He should have been back by now."

"Oh, yeah? How long's he been gone?" When Carmine didn't answer after a few seconds, Louie said, "Hey, I asked you a question. How come you don't answer? You always do that. You say sumpin', I ask a question, you never answer."

Carmine muttered.

Still nettled, Louie said, "He probably . . . I don't know, he's just running, that's all."

Carmine looked at his watch again, tapped the dashboard, and blew another bubble. Then he laughed to himself, pulled the lever out of park, and with two quick maneuvers, tapping the cars in front and behind, swung out onto the street, tires chirping as he pulled away.

"Where the hell we going?" Louie asked.

They were at the foot of the hill before Carmine answered. "Let's take a little spin out to Oak Way Cemetery."

Harold Parkins sat and stared at the wall in the basement of the chapel and then looked back at the clock on the wall behind him over the old oak desk. It had been just over an hour, an hour of cooling. An hour was on the low safe side. An hour and a half, two hours, were better, but if you knew what you were doing, were careful, you could even open up right away. He'd done it a few times when rushed. Didn't like to, but it could be done. Thing was, he didn't like Alex telling him his job, telling him what to do.

Putting on his leather work gloves, Harold got up slowly. This was the first since he'd done that kid but this one shouldn't bother him. It was a swap. No problem there. Could do swaps all day. Could do them standing on his head. Only trouble was that they were tough on the arms and he'd done five legit jobs today already. Three in the morning, two in the afternoon.

He positioned the rectangular barrel against the wall under the door and got the broom and the rake ready. A reddish-brown paste had congealed under the door and oozed a few inches down the wall. He would have to do some scraping for this one.

He opened the door and stood back for a moment away from the rush of heat and the smell. Actually, the smell wasn't bad, just, just . . . characteristic.

Harold chewed on his cheek and peered in. Everything was intact but would probably break up when he put the rake to it.

He hooked the rake under the jawbone and pulled. The whole thing started to follow and then quivered and fell apart. He flicked the skull out and into the barrel. A few more flicks skidded out the rib cage, pelvic structure, arms and legs.

There wasn't much to this one. She'd been small, all wizened up, and would probably be brittle as hell. That was good. Easy on the arms.

He dragged the barrel around the corner, and reached in for the skull. It was on the small side, but other than that pretty much the same as any other. You've seen one skull, you've seen them all. Except for the teeth. You really got a look at the old choppers this way. This old gal still had quite a few teeth, mostly on the top, kind of surprising for a ninety-three-year-old. Harold ran his tongue around his mouth, feeling the gaps. Although he had bridgework, he seldom wore it. He never could get used to the feel of it.

Harold gently put the skull on the cement table, its edges built up like the lips of a tray. He opened and closed his fingers a few times to limber them before reaching down for the mallet. Actually, the mallet looked like a bathroom plunger except that its head was cement rather than rubber.

Damn, how long had he been doing this? Over twenty-five years now. Not these kinds of jobs, of course. These were recent. Just a few years. But legitimately he'd been cooking and cracking a mighty long time. And he was good at it. He knew that. It wasn't just anyone who could do this. There was a lot more to it than setting a few dials and gauges and waiting around.

Sometimes things wouldn't go right and you had to start over, do some propping up of the cadaver with a bundle of newspapers so it would burn easily. Might just as likely be a bunch of old Boston *Globes* setting on some mantel as Uncle Frank or Aunt Sally. At least partly. Who the hell knew?

Harold was the only one to do this work regularly. Sometimes he got a little help, but most of the others just didn't have the stomach for it. He knew Alex didn't. Alex liked to act as if he could do this real easy but, because he was a nice guy, he performed a favor and let Harold.

The thing was, you had to remember that this had been a person and show some respect. Harold always remembered. He always showed respect. That was what was wrong with Alex lately. Alex didn't care about anyone but Alex. The girl or the young kid hadn't bothered Alex at all because he didn't have to be down here with them and the ovens and then afterward doing this.

Harold put the dust mask over his nose and mouth. You had to be careful about breathing in too much bone dust. Who the hell knew what that could cause a few years down the line? You heard all the time about people like coal miners or construction workers having problems because of what they breathed in on the job.

Hefting the mallet, Harold sighed. Even when he was through here, he wasn't finished for the night. With a swap, you weren't finished until you had scattered the ashes. Alex didn't want them scattered here in the cemetery anymore or tossed in the pond, so that meant he'd have to take them someplace and throw them into the wind, or dump them into the Charles. It was too bad. They were terrific for shrubs.

When Peter heard the rush of footsteps behind him, he pivoted quickly, swinging the crowbar, feeling it strike, hearing the heavy, soft thud. But the momentum of the stocky man carried him into Peter, knocking him to the ground, where they grappled, arms and legs flailing wildly.

The crowbar caught Alex in the upper arm but his heavy jacket absorbed much of the force. He tried to position himself on top of Peter, to pin him so that he could deliver a crippling or killing blow to the head or windpipe. Peter had lost hold of the crowbar when he had swung it and it had arced into the bushes someplace.

Peter squirmed under the weight of the burly man astride him. His arms were pinned by Alex's knees but his legs were free and he tried to bring his knee up for a groin shot or just to topple him. Already, Alex's breathing was short and labored and Peter felt that this was his best hope, that his own conditioning would allow him to outlast this antagonist and break free.

Suddenly, Alex yelled out three names and Peter knew he was calling for reinforcements. In desperation, he arched and twisted his body, kicking his foot up and catching Alex in the side of the head, but the cushioned soles had little effect.

"You son of a bitch," Alex croaked, slamming his fist into Peter's cheek. Peter swung his legs again, felt Alex shift a bit, and started to slip free. The pressure on his arms released and he sprung his fist up and felt it strike something hard, maybe the chin. He swung again, hit again, and started to gain the advantage. He was off the ground, pushing the burly man back, glancing into the bushes for the crowbar, when they were on him from behind. He felt himself being driven back to the ground and then everything went black.

As they carried Peter to the chapel, Alex pondered the coincidence of two runners—first that girl and now this person—stumbling upon them as they did their work at night. Then he wondered whether this one had come out here alone. Runners often ran together. Maybe there was someone else out there.

"Hurry up," he said to the two lugging Peter's inert form. He rubbed his upper arm where the crowbar had gotten him. The pain was beginning to blossom.

They carried Peter down the stairs, bouncing him a little, like a cumbersome sack. They dropped him on the floor behind the twin ovens as Alex darted around looking for the rolling table. He found it in an anteroom, wheeled it out, and the other two lifted Peter onto it.

Alex examined Peter carefully. He was unconscious and looked as though he would be for some time. He should kill him now and would if he had a gun or knife but it didn't matter if Harold got him right into the oven. Trouble was that Harold was getting squeamish.

"Harold! Get your ass out here."

Harold slowly came from around the corner where he had been finishing with knocking and grinding the tough pelvic bones into powder and chips.

"Get this one in right away, you hear me? He saw us outside."

Harold's mouth was slack, his eyes blank. He looked terrible, Alex thought. It was funny how he hadn't noticed that Harold had lost weight.

"You hear what I just said?"

Alex was about to repeat when Harold finally nodded.

"Matter of fact, let's get him in right now." Alex stepped to one of the oven doors, touched the handle, and jerked his hand back. The door was still hot.

Harold's face came to life, regained its thinking ways. "I can do it. I know how to do my job."

Alex stood back, sucked his singed finger, and regarded Harold carefully. Maybe Harold was all right now. At least he was talking, showing some life.

"Okay, you get him in right away, before he comes to. If he does." Alex was anxious to get back out to see whether there was anyone else out there skulking around and to check whether this one had left a car outside anyplace. He could be back in a few minutes to check that Harold was doing his job.

He turned to the others. "Let's get back out." As they climbed the stairs, he instructed them to scour the cemetery for other snoopers.

Then he had a doubt. He sent the others on their way and went back down to the basement. He looked in where Peter lay on the table, felt reassured, and darted back out.

Harold had the oven door open and was beginning to fiddle with the gauges.

Harold sat behind the old oak desk staring at the wall, at the ovens, at the form on the steel table. Alex was going to be angry with him if he didn't get moving soon, get the job done. But that didn't make sense because he had already done the job. That was what was wrong; he had done this job before, twice before, and he couldn't do it again.

He wouldn't be able to sleep if he did it again and he couldn't stand that. That and spilling his guts all over the place until there was nothing left but the pain.

He looked at the form on the table, in a way glad now that he knew what was wrong, knew why what Alex had just said didn't make any sense. Alex told him to put this one in the oven but he already had. He stared at the form and it was the girl and then it was the young boy, so what Alex told him to do made no sense, no sense to be told to do what you have already done.

A string of spittle ran from the corner of Harold's slack mouth and dripped unnoticed onto his blue work shirt. What he should be doing was what Alex had interrupted him at. He should be getting the ashes and bone chips ready to put in the little cardboard box so that he could throw them into the wind and water.

The figure on the table moaned, opened its eyes, and looked about, frightened and incomprehending. Harold blinked and stared and suddenly saw that it wasn't the girl or the young boy.

No, it wasn't them. It was . . . it was Alex. Harold's surprise changed to a great hatred and he stood up quickly, knocking his chair back and over. Yes, it was Alex stirring on that table, getting ready to roll off. Why hadn't he noticed that it was Alex? Alex who had made him do those things to the pretty girl and the young boy.

If there was one thing he knew now, it was that he hated Alex. Alex had made him so that he couldn't sleep those nights, so that he couldn't hold food half the time.

And now he knew what he would do. Let's see how Alex liked it there in the oven, the nice hot oven that turned you to a little pile of ashes.

When Peter opened his eyes, he was at first confused but then quickly remembered his struggle of a few minutes ago and knew that the wild-eyed figure coming at him from behind the old desk meant him no good.

He slid from the table, groggy and unsteady, and as Harold charged with groping, clumsy arms, Peter lowered his head and threw his shoulder hard into Harold's middle. He was surprised at how easily the older man fell back into the brick wall, painted a pale green, and collapsed to the floor. Peter poised his fist and then held back. The old man sat, staring, drooling, and helpless.

Peter stood, trying to clear his head and assess his situation. He looked from the sagging Harold to the oven, heard the rush of flame and heat meant for him. He thought of Alison and shook his head in rejection of the image of what had happened to her.

He looked down at Harold again. Here, more than likely, was the person who had killed Alison. An enormous repulsion and loathing filled him. He bent down, his face close to Harold's, clutched his shirt and slid his hands to Harold's throat but there was no resistance. Peter stood up quickly. He wanted to get away from this disgusting man, this disgusting place.

He looked about for some sort of weapon. He skipped to the little corridor running beside the ovens, saw the table, messy with white powder and chips, and the mallet standing beside it. He picked up the mallet, grimacing as he imagined its purpose, and bounced back out to Harold, still slumped and salivating. But now he was crying too.

Opposite the short corridor where he had picked up the mallet, on the other side of the crematory ovens, was the doorway Peter had been brought in through. Cautiously, the short, heavy mallet poised in front of him, he stepped into another room, larger than the one he had left.

On shelves behind glass, rather like china closets, were urns neatly arranged and labeled. He wondered about them briefly as he slipped from the room into a large basement filled with cemetery paraphernalia, evidently an area of storage and maintenance: lawn mowers, plastic-sod rolls, a small dump truck. He searched for an exit, saw a staircase and climbed carefully, listening, feeling the pain in his head beginning to intensify.

At the top of the stairs, he stepped into the chapel itself, near the altar. He could see only one exit, at the end of the aisle running down between two rows of pews.

Staying near the wall, he ran down a side aisle toward the

exit and was almost at it when the door opened. He dropped to the floor beside the last pew and watched the man who had knocked him to the ground outside come in followed by a huge man. He recognized the huge man's face immediately; he had driven the Pontiac that had nicked his leg.

"There should be practically nothing left of him by now," the smaller man was saying, "except bones."

The big man was looking all around and suddenly came right at Peter, drawing for his revolver under his coat. Peter sprang to his feet, dove straight at Carmine, and stunned him with a blow square in the chest with the mallet. He pushed past him and the startled Alex and was almost through the door when the bullet burned a furrow along the back of his right leg.

Heedless of the searing pain, he jumped down the three cement steps, ran straight across the narrow road, glimpsing the old pickup truck parked a few feet away. He pushed through a border of tall yews, his shoes plunging through the crust of snow on the other side. Immediately, he realized his mistake and knew he had to get back on a road. Running in the snow was impossible and he made a perfect target against its backdrop.

He heard yelling behind him back by the chapel and the heavy, flat bark of the pistol. The cemetery was crisscrossed with paths and roads and quickly he was on plowed pavement again. He had to get to the fence. Once over it, they'd never catch him.

He turned left, toward the fence, and sprinted up the path, a steep winding incline. He was almost to the road that looped the circumference of the cemetery and the tall, spiked fence that lay beyond it when he heard the roar of the pickup truck and saw its headlights through the shrubs and trees heading toward him.

Just as he hit the circumference road and was going to cross it to the fence, the truck swung around the corner, its lights throwing his long, bobbing shadow ahead. Instantly, he sprang back into the snow, off the road, seeking cover of shrubbery and gravestones.

The truck swung in his direction, trying to pick him up in its headlights. A single shot rang out.

Running as fast as he could manage in the snow, Peter sped down a sharp dip into a heavily wooded little gully, dark with shadows and overgrowth. Pausing beside an enormous oak, he listened for the truck. Nothing. His head throbbed and his leg, where the bullet had creased it, burned. He felt the leg. It was sticky but not bleeding heavily as far as he could tell. He had lost his running gloves and hat and knew the cold would soon be a problem. Now, faintly, he heard the truck circling the area where he had gone in.

Moving cautiously, trying to stay under cover as much as possible, he pulled himself up the other side of the gully, looked carefully from side to side, and crossed a small path. Two roads to cross and he'd be at the fence. He wondered whether the big man with the gun was on foot. He'd have to be watchful.

He pushed ahead, crossed the first road, and stopped beside a pine tree. There was no sign of the truck. He squinted into the dark. The moon was covered by a small cloud. Ahead about two hundred feet, the fence glinted dully in the street-lamps.

He moved toward it. At the circumference road, he looked quickly both ways and then crossed the thirty feet to the fence. He grasped the cold metal and pulled himself upward, feet pawing the thin spikes. His hand clutched the top crossbar, above which jutted the sharp spikes. As he attempted to raise his wounded leg to the crossbar, he sagged and fell back onto the snow. He stared up at the lethal series of spires.

Then he heard the truck coming fast. He jumped for the top crossbar, pulling slowly and deliberately while his feet pushed and slid against the black rods. He swung his legs up so that he was lying beside the crossbar as he clung to it.

When the truck plowed through the snow and up to the fence, he pushed upward with hands and feet, and was almost over when he felt Carmine's huge hand strangle his ankle and pull him back down to the crusted snow.

"Hey, English teacher, you goin' somewhere?" Carmine's grinning face was close to Peter's. Effortlessly, he picked Peter up and slammed him into the fence. Still grinning, he regarded Peter closely.

"Yeah, you're going someplace. You're going right back to where you came from. That's not too bad, is it? It's nice and warm back there." Carmine laughed at his irony. He thought it was clever.

Alex was now beside them. "Take care of this guy right now before we bring him back," he said.

Carmine gave Alex a quick, condescending look. "Not here. Too close to the street. Besides, teacher here has been a real pain in the ass to me. I want him to think about where he's going for a few minutes."

He yanked Peter from the fence, jacked Peter's arms high up behind his back, and pushed him roughly across the snow to the truck.

Bracing himself against the pain shooting through his shoulder joints, Peter twisted and kicked back hard at Carmine's shins, feeling his running shoes strike ineffectually.

Carmine laughed and pulled up harder on Peter's arms. Peter's eyes watered with pain as he was shoved into the cab of the truck.

They rode back to the chapel, Alex driving, Peter in the middle, and Carmine beside him, grinning widely, his magnum pressed into the side of Peter's neck.

Peter tried to calm his racing mind, to force some plan of escape. He knew he was lucky he hadn't been killed outright before being brought back, that only Carmine's pleasure at toying with him was postponing his execution, which would probably come suddenly with no preliminaries either when they got out of the truck or when he was back down by the ovens.

Alex stopped the truck by the door to the chapel. Carmine got out, keeping the revolver on Peter. "Let's go," he said.

Slowly, Peter got out. He knew there was no chance to bolt. Carmine had the magnum pressed into his stomach. He thought of the bullet that had grazed his leg but could no longer feel any pain there. At any moment he expected to feel his belly blown open. He couldn't run, but he had to do something. He could talk, maybe stall. But for what? he wondered.

"You were driving the car that hit me on Charles Street," he said, surprised at how calm and matter-of-fact his voice sounded.

Carmine smiled and probed the magnum into Peter's stomach. "You don't think that I couldn't have really got you if I wanted to, do you?"

"But why?"

"Don't play innocent with me," Carmine snarled, pushing Peter toward the chapel, then grabbing tightly on to his sweat suit before he could try to run.

Alex led them downstairs. He muttered something when he saw Harold, eyes glazed, sprawled against the wall. He nudged him with his boot and turned to Carmine. "We ought to take care of him too. He's good for nothing and no one will ever miss him."

Carmine shrugged noncommittally. He was more interested in Peter.

"Okay, you nosy bastard," he said, coming close to Peter, the magnum, huge in his hand, pointing at Peter's chest.

Peter swung his head at a gurgling, animal sound to his left and saw Harold, a wild man, face contorted, pinioning Alex, pushing him to the wall, toward the ovens. Despite his burliness, Alex seemed like a child in the desperate, insane strength of Harold's frenzy.

Instantly, Peter recognized that Carmine's distraction might be his only chance. Hunching his shoulder, he flung his body at Carmine's legs, at the knees, catching him off balance, and drove him back.

Dropping his arms to his sides to brace against toppling, Carmine leaned back against the door of the oven, yowling enormously as its heat seared through his clothing.

Seeing a chance, Peter drove his head into probably the only vulnerable spot on the giant body.

Carmine dropped to his knees, his face blue with double pain: the heat that sizzled his back and the crippling waves of agony that welled from his lower belly.

Peter pulled back, frantically looking for the magnum. He couldn't see it; it wasn't in Carmine's hand. Probably, the big man was sitting on it.

Suddenly, Harold, still gurgling animal sounds, was astride Carmine, oblivious to him. One arm was wrapped around Alex's throat, the other pulled at the insulated handle of the oven door, releasing a gush of terrible heat.

Alex screamed, his rolling eyes wide and imploring. In an instant, Harold had Alex aloft in both arms, ready to heave him into the inferno.

"No!" Peter screeched as he plunged at Harold's ankles, toppling him and Alex to the floor.

Peter slithered beside the still-moaning Carmine looking for the magnum. It was pinned under Carmine's thigh. As he started to pull it free, Carmine swung his arm in a huge backhanded sweep, knocking Peter back.

The magnum lay between them.

They dove for it together and white waves flashed through Peter's head at the collision. Other waves too, waves of realization that he had had a chance and blew it, sickened him, and he thought he was going to black out.

The blast of gunshot, then another, jolted him but he felt no pain.

With the echoes of the shots still ringing in his ears, he opened his eyes and saw Carmine slumped back, his eyes wide, staring, and sightless. Harold and Alex lay in a tumble and Lieutenant Gabriel and two uniformed officers bent down anxiously to him.

CHAPTER 19

Peter watched Clark sniff a strand of tinsel and then bat a low ornament on the small tree in the front window. They sat, he, Nancy, and Lieutenant Gabriel, with coffee in Peter's living room brightened by the midmorning sun.

"What we'll ultimately get them on or even *who* we will ultimately get is hard to say at this point, Mr. Swann," Lieutenant Gabriel said. "We know who was involved now, and what they were doing, but pinning it on the top guys might be tough."

He offered his pack of Pall Malls around. Nancy took one. He held the match for her and lit his own. Clark tested the air and left the room in measured steps, maintaining his dignity.

"However, thanks to you, we will put a pretty slick and pretty gruesome scheme out of operation."

"The thanks go to you, Lieutenant. Talk about the nick of time." Peter shuddered as he remembered. "And I appreciate your coming by to fill us in on the loose ends."

Lieutenant Gabriel looked at Nancy, hesitating. "It's not pleasant, Miss Brewer. But I imagine Mr. Swann has told you what happened to Miss Bradley."

"It's horrible. I can't imagine . . ."

"Apparently," Lieutenant Gabriel said, "the original purpose of the whole deal was to store goods on speculation. For example, drugs that don't readily perish if stored properly. Cocaine, primarily. This business of speculation, by the way, is highly unusual. Organized crime generally moves things immediately, for a number of reasons, one of which is the problem of a suitable place to hide whatever they are dealing with. I guess this time they thought they had the perfect place, and would have if it wasn't for you, Mr. Swann."

"That's the part I don't understand," Nancy said.

"It's simple." Lieutenant Gabriel dragged deeply on his Pall Mall, letting the smoke slowly trickle from his mouth and nose as he spoke. "They would use caskets to store anything they thought might appreciate in value. Drugs, as I have mentioned. Art objects, jewelry, silverware taken in house breaks."

"Mrs. Beauchesne's Royal Doulton could very well be buried out there. She's my neighbor, sweet old lady," Peter said to Lieutenant Gabriel.

"After a funeral," Lieutenant Gabriel continued, "if there was something to store, they would simply remove the body, dispose of it by cremation, and use the casket. Naturally, activity by them around the grave site looked perfectly normal."

Lieutenant Gabriel sipped his coffee. "It was probably later that they hit on the idea of using cremation as a means of getting rid of the bodies of underworld contracts. Really clever. Not a trace."

Nancy started to say something, stopped, breathed in deeply from her cigarette, and started again, her voice bumpy. "So Alison was . . . I still don't . . ."

Peter and Lieutenant Gabriel began to speak together.

"Excuse me, Mr. Swann, let me." Lieutenant Gabriel's voice was gentle as he spoke to Nancy. "Normally they did their work during the day, I imagine, when no passerby would look twice at what they might be doing. Miss Bradley stumbled upon them after dark and, being curious, investigated. They couldn't afford a witness."

"But her car?" Nancy said.

Lieutenant Gabriel shrugged. "Car shredder. Anything. Cars are easily disposed of."

They sat through a few moments of silence. Lieutenant Gabriel finished his coffee and stood up. "Well, I should be going." He extended his hand. "Thanks again, Mr. Swann. By the way, how's the leg?"

Peter dismissed it with a wave of his hand. "Fine."

At the door, Lieutenant Gabriel paused. "I don't like to bring in a spoiler, but just play it cool, huh, Mr. Swann? You'll have police protection for a while because you'll have to do some testifying." He smiled. "You have screwed up the works for some pretty powerful people. Just how much you have screwed them up we'll know later. We haven't finished digging yet."

Peter let Lieutenant Gabriel out and went back to Nancy. It was two days before Christmas and she had taken the day off to do some shopping with him.

She put her cup to one side on the coffee table when he sat beside her on the old cushiony sofa. She leaned her head back and neither spoke for several moments. He knew she was deeply bothered by what had happened to Alison.

"It's a wicked, wicked world, Nance, old girl," he said finally.

She sniffled. "Don't make light of it, Peter."

"I'm not," he said softly, taking her hand.

"God, it could have been you. I mean, you came pretty close."

Peter thought of Alex, Carmine, Harold. Of the ovens. He squeezed her hand and then kissed her gently. "Come on," he said, "let's do some shopping and try to forget all this. At least for now. Let's think of Christmas."

They put on their coats and went outside to her car. As he locked the door, he wondered whether he would have a police tail. At least it would be easier to take than the one he had had the past few days, the one he had never been able to spot.

CHAPTER 20

When Peter had finished speaking, they sat in silence for several minutes. Outside, a light snow was falling. They were at Doug's place and Peter had told him everything, uneuphemistically but as gently as he could. It had been a dreaded but necessary task. Doug deserved no less than the total truth.

Finally, Doug got up and went to the window. For some time he stared out at a world making ready for the happiest yet the saddest of holidays. When he sat down again, his eye was clear and his voice was steady.

"That was quite a chance you took, Peter. One doesn't take on the mob lightly." Peter had minimized his own role but Doug saw through the understatement.

"Doug, you of all people know what I mean when I say that Alison meant as much to me as to you. In a different way, but no less intense."

"Whatever the motivation, it was a very brave . . ." His voice faltered; he seemed very tired.

"Doug, for my money you wrote the book on bravery. I am living testimony to that."

They sat in silence again, neither wanting the mood or the conversation to become maudlin.

Peter went to Doug and placed a hand on his shoulder. "On Christmas, I know you'll want to be with your family, but if you get a chance come to my place and spend some time with Nancy and me."

Doug nodded. "Thank you. That would be nice." He turned from Peter suddenly and went into the bathroom. Peter heard water running.

Peter sat by himself for a few minutes. The water stopped running in the bathroom. Now that the intensity of effort and tension born from the involvement of finding out, of risking himself, was over, the full horror of what had happened to Alison reached the bloom of emotional as well as intellectual awareness.

He wondered how Doug would live with it.

He wondered how he would live with it.

Lieutenant Gabriel had warned of possible retribution by those he had put out of business but he doubted it would happen. For one thing, they were usually very careful to make connections between themselves and their operatives tenuous at best and retaliation would only serve to confirm that connection. He wasn't sure that really made sense but he preferred to believe it. It was reassuring.

There *was* a small measure of comfort in knowing that he had done some damage to a malignant system but that was tempered by knowing that it merely put a cramp in their style. Still, you do what you can.

He got up and started to go to Doug but stopped. Doug needed to be alone. Later, he could help more. And he would.

He let himself out. He wanted Nancy now very badly. He scuffed powdery snow as he walked to the Jaguar and lifted his face to the clean, cold stings of the swirling flakes. Walking like this, looking up at diving snowflakes, trying to follow the flight of just one, seeing if he could get it to hit his eye, was something he had done as a kid.

At the car, he brushed the snow from the windshield before getting in and looked up at the falling flakes again. They seemed faster and heavier now. It would be a white Christmas.

ABOUT THE AUTHOR

William L. Story is a high school teacher who was born and raised in Salem, Massachusetts. He is the author of short stories which have been published in *Mike Shayne Mystery Magazine* and one previous novel, *Domino Spill*. *Cemeteries Are for Dying* is his first novel for the Crime Club. Mr. Story lives with his wife and two children in Peabody, Massachusetts.